THE SPHERE OF INFINITY

THE SPHERE OF INFINITY

AN ALADDIN RETELLING NOVELLA

DAY LEITAO

SPARKLY WAVE

Cover illustration by Natalya Sorokina (Jwitless)

ISBN: 978-1-9992427-0-1

CONTENTS

FREEBIES!

Sign up and get this and another ebook for free

https://dayleitao.com

You'll also get news, scoops, more freebies, book recommendations, chances to enter giveaways, and more!

PROLOGUE

THE HUMAN UNIVERSE

Time erases memory. Facts become legend and truths get lost in the tunnel of time. If Humanity was given a second chance and went on to occupy two neighbor galaxies, it was thanks to two races who taught them interplanetary travel and showed them how to find Earth-like planets.

But that was a long time ago. Contact was cut, and the humans called their benefactor races simply the Blues. In this Human Universe, there was a planet, Samitri. Now, this is human legend, and the accounts are inaccurate at best, plain ludicrous at worst. This planet had been inhabited by large reptiles that the humans soon called dragons, reminded of their legendary creatures. They lived in peace with humans, and could even communicate with them. Some special humans could even control these creatures.

But that was the stuff of legend. Samitri was a very different place now.

1
———

THE BLACK MOUSE

Alana clutched the information capsule in her hands. Done. She put it in her heart-shaped necklace locket. Easy. This was a battered old ship and it was hard to imagine why anyone would want any information from here, but that was none of her business. She should be glad that there were still things to be stolen in Samitri's spaceship port. Perhaps less than before, but at least enough to keep her busy. And it was not surprising that as fewer and fewer rich people—or people, for any matter—visited her planet, the smaller the jobs were getting. Alana sighed. Eventually, this spring would dry up—but this was not the time to think about it.

While she opened the door to the lower compartment, a red light flickered. No, no, no. That wasn't supposed to happen. How could this old junk have an inner alarm system? Still, she glided through the luggage compartment and searched for the gap between the landing gears. Nobody should expect that gap to be used as an escape, for the simple reason that it was impossible—at least for most adults. Thin, short, tiny, and with a small frame, Alana was no bigger than many 10-standard-year-old children. It was her greatest advantage. She glanced outside and her stomach dropped. Why were all these guards on patrol tonight? Wait. She'd heard something about some big shot leader from Ringon arriving. Why today?

Her grumbling hadn't even finished when she realized that the ridiculous amount of guards wasn't the worst: a siren blared and all doors to the port were being closed automatically. This task was getting worse by the minute, and it wasn't even that well paid. Alana gulped. Well, she couldn't expect to come in and out of the docks stealing things in the night and never be caught. As silently as she could, Alana slid out of the ship. There was one way out, through the gap beneath one of the gates. The issue would be ensuring no guards would spot her. Maybe she could deal with one or two, though.

Moving from beneath one ship to the other, she got close to the gate with the tiny gap—large enough for her. Two guards secured it. Idiots. The gate was shut. They should be searching the port for her, not standing here. She pulled a nut and threw it far away from her. The guards just looked and shrugged. Great.

Fine, they wanted it the hard way, they'd have to do it the hard way. She pulled down her hood, covered her face, jumped close to them, pointed her taser gun at a guard, and shot. He dropped to the ground. Alana got up, shot the other, and slid through the gap as she heard a multitude of steps approaching her. This wasn't good. Wasn't good at all.

Alana ran as fast as she could towards the city. Either she found a place to hide, or soon she'd be caught. She reached the market with its abandoned booths and found an empty wooden box for her to hide in. They shouldn't look for her there, since it was too small. Eyes closed in the darkness, she slowed her breathing and focused on quieting her heart.

Steps echoed in the distance, then very close, and then she heard inner space hovers flying. Wow, some operation they were having. Time passed and the sounds didn't fade. The head of security must have been really interested in causing a good impression. Nobody usually cared about simple thieves who didn't even steal anything. She hadn't stolen anything, really, just copied some information. Nothing was missing. And it wasn't as if she'd been in the Grand Palace, collecting government information; it was just a stupid private spaceship, and it wasn't even fancy. Still, someone wanted to put on a show. Never mind. The market would open in the morning, and in the hustle and bustle of its movement, she'd find her opportunity to escape. All she had to do was survive a night folded in a tiny box. No big deal. Alana exhaled as she realized the worst had been over.

Catching her for her crime would not even be the worst. The problem was that in her planet, Samitri, every citizen, or rather, every common citizen, not counting the government officials, visitors, and farm owners, had a chip identifying them, from where all their movements were controlled. Alana had escaped when they'd first gathered everyone to implant their chips. Not even her mother believed that she could evade the authorities for more than a day. She'd been evading them for four standard years now, or since she'd been twelve.

Avoiding walking outside during the day, she found herself a source of income in Samitri's Blood Tavern, where she got her leads and little jobs from the same person who had once employed her father. She became the Black Mouse, a small boy expert on coming in and out of tight places, stealing information and sometimes small objects. They had no idea she was a girl, and no idea who she was, but as long as she finished her contracts, nobody really cared. Alana clutched the locket holding the information. Despite everything, she'd managed to bring it.

Her body was getting stiff, but her pursuers still hadn't given up. Well, she knew it would be a long night, and should be glad that even though she was in a tiny box, she was still free. A sound startled her as the top cover was pulled up. No, no, no. Now she was trapped. Trapped like a mouse. Or maybe not. She quickly pulled her taser. Her strategy would be to tase her captor and make a run for it. The face that appeared through the opening was not what she'd expected, though. It was a young man with calm blue eyes and very white, sandy hair. The eyes got her and cost her escape because in her hesitation he grabbed her taser. Alana's heart was about to explode.

The prospect of being sent to a penal colony and abandoning her mother tore her apart. Her mother, that was what her thoughts turned to, as she faced the strange young man. He stared at her in silence, put a finger over his lips, deactivated her taser and returned it to her. Activating it again wouldn't be such a big deal, but she couldn't stop staring at him. His face was not that clear against the lights from above, but there was something memorable in it.

He closed the cover and his steps sounded further and further. Was he going to tell someone else? Get help? Should she make a run for it? Her impression was that he wanted to help her, but maybe it was only her imagination because he was so good looking. As if she'd even seen him properly. While Alana mentally debated if she should remain there or make a run for it, the sounds around the market quieted. Even the hovers stopped flying. Could it be a trap? There would be no reason for that, as the young man could have taken her when he'd found her. He could have even tased her. And yet he hadn't. Alana had no idea why.

Peeking out of her box, she found the area around her empty and walked slowly away from it, throwing her cloak in a small garbage can. Her clothes were now black instead of grey, and different from before. Walking slowly was a better strategy not to call attention, not that it helped much. If someone stopped and asked for identification, she'd still be in trouble, but then, she could deal with one or two people, even three.

As she reached the street where she lived, someone jumped from a roof in front of her: the white-haired boy.

He stared at her in curiosity—or something else she couldn't quite understand—and asked, "Who are you?"

Her hands had been in her pocket, where the taser gun was. She realized with regret that she wasn't wearing goggles or glasses and he could see her hazel green eyes. But then, probably a quarter of the population in Samitri had dark skin and green eyes like hers, except that her skin was lighter since it didn't get as much sunlight. She'd be more careful from now on and never remove her goggles. At least her enormous, bushy brown hair was under a hood.

Alana wished life were very different, wished she could talk to him, wished he hadn't been following her as a criminal to be caught. She understood why boys could make girls lose their minds. But she couldn't lose hers. Her fingers pressed the taser trigger. His eyes registered shock and betrayal for a second before he collapsed forward. She caught him mid-fall, turned him, and placed him carefully on the ground so that he wouldn't get hurt.

She touched his almost white hair. "I'm sorry. I just can't risk getting caught. But I think you're nice and trying to help me. And you're really cute. Sorry."

Knowing he was unconscious gave her the courage to say all of that. There was something a little odd about him. Hair and eyelashes were too blond, and his skin was too pale. She'd certainly never seen him before. Was he a new guard? If only her life had been different, she would have loved to get to know him. As it was, she turned around and walked home.

———

JASPER OPENED HIS EYES. The girl hadn't managed to knock him out completely, and he got up while her steps echoed in the distance. He turned around and decided to head back to the palace on his own when he heard steps approaching him.

Max, the chief of security, was beside him, out of breath. "Sir, I was told not to leave you alone. Sir."

"Then don't tell anyone you left me alone."

Max's face was blank as if measuring the possibilities.

Jasper added, "Also, if I were you, I wouldn't let anyone know that there has been a problem with security. Just say that it was a false alarm. I won't tell anyone about this and I suggest you do the same."

Max still just stared as if unsure.

Jasper smiled, "Hey, it's been a fun night. I think you can take me back to the palace."

Max nodded. He looked ashamed, and he'd better be. These Samitri guards tried to make a spectacle of their security and couldn't even deal with a young girl. Plus soft Jasper, who'd been sent to Samitri to toughen up, did the work a bunch of grown men couldn't. He'd used his hunting skills to find the girl. Not that he hunted, but he rescued hurt animals, animals who were afraid and thought he was their enemy, who stared at him with pleading, fearful eyes, unaware he was their friend—like the girl. Not that he had been planning on helping anyone. He had no idea what he'd been planning other than finding something to do. But then, her eyes had gotten him. There was innocence, fear, and something else in them. The only thing he didn't understand was why she was running, but he didn't understand this planet anyway.

———

"Came home late last night?"

Alana's mother typed in the kitchen, sitting on her manual wheelchair, and didn't seem worried.

"A little," Alana replied. "More security than usual. I had to make sure I wasn't followed." She had been followed, though, and had he not revealed himself to her, he could have perhaps found her address. The worst was that if she'd been caught, at this very moment she could be in prison instead of home. She'd have to be more careful.

Her mother turned to her. "Darling, don't you think this is enough? You could try to escape, go somewhere else. There's no future for you here."

Indeed. Alana's greatest dream was to go to Ringon, the planet where the Human Universe government stood. While she despised that government, she knew Ringon was a place where people could dream and be whatever they wanted, unlike in Samitri, where every able citizen had to work on the farms. But it wasn't that simple. "I'm not leaving you, mom."

Her mother sighed. "You're young. You can still craft your future."

"We'll leave together."

Her mother had a faint smile and turned back to her writing. She'd been hurt in the Fifth Battle when Samitri thought it was fighting for independence. Independence! Instead of being ruled by a monarchy who took an insane amount of taxes, they became ruled by the Peace Alliance. They didn't take any taxes, for the simple reason that the pay was so low that people could barely afford to eat. Previous owners of small properties were forced into labor, and only big farms remained. Samitri, once a prosperous farming and tourism planet, with a lively market and rich farmers, became a planet of contrasts. On one side, the rich government and a few farm owners, and on the other, in misery, the rest of the population. Alana lived in a small house with a tiny bedroom and a kitchen.

Her mother, because of her disability, wasn't forced to work. She wrote for a living, or sort of. She actually sold her novels and stories to an editor who was happy to pretend to pay her more than she did. That way, her mother could use the money Alana made with her small tasks, and they at least always had enough to eat and even sometimes to give to their neighbors and friends. For that reason, Alana never regretted stealing, which was one of the few things she'd learned from her father. Despite her mother's protests, he had taught Alana the ins and outs of the job. Killed when Samitri revolted against the new government, at least her father had given Alana a way to survive—and enough resilience and courage to hope.

Her mother's stories were romantic in nature, with extremely good looking men who came to rescue poor damsels. She'd always advised Alana that they were a bunch of junk, made so people would forget the reality they lived in and stop fighting. Alana sometimes read them when her mother wasn't watching, though. Yes, it would be silly to hope that someone would save her, but those were just stories, right? And in one thing her mother had been wrong. She always said that nobody was as good looking as in the stories, but the young man who'd almost caught her that night would surely fit one of her descriptions, except maybe for the too light hair.

But what Alana wished was not a handsome young man. Her savior would be a large amount of credits. With that, she would be able to run away and even fix her mother's legs. None of her past would matter. More than ever, she was sure that money was the solution to everything. All she hoped was for a breakthrough opportunity to leave her survival cycle.

2

JASPER

Jasper looked at the scenery from the balcony of the Samitri Palace. Apart from the city where most workers lived, there was a lot of green. From there, trains took them to work in the morning and brought them back in the afternoon. The governor's daughter, Leah, stood by his side. She was a very beautiful girl, with brown hair and eyes and skin gold like river sand, but there was something artificial in her. Perhaps it was just that Jasper indeed preferred to spend time with animals than with people. At least they were honest.

Jasper had a question. "Why don't you use droids?"

"In the farms? There is a lot of automation already, but we wouldn't replace our people with droids. You can't produce the best laski meat in the Human Universe by using droids. And it was important to assure that the people from the planet kept their jobs and their tradition. They're proud of what they do, you see?"

"I want to see one of those farms. Can you take me there?"

Leah had a bright, happy smile. "Sure."

Jasper got his sunglasses, hat, cloak, and special gloves. He loved nature so much and yet had to hide from daylight.

THERE WERE two fences around a large pasture with a dozen or so laskis. The large creatures seemed happier than their counterparts in Ringon, which were confined to tight spaces. Neither their claws nor their horns had been removed, which was also nice.

One laski approached the inner fence. Jasper climbed over the outer fence and approached it. Leah screamed his name but he ignored as he stepped in and touched the creature's magnificent horns and felt how soft its blue skin was despite its thickness. One day that skin would be someone's coat, boot, or pants. Well, at least they used everything from the laskis. Such a beautiful beast with a due date to die.

He walked back to Leah, and she put her hands over her heart. "Don't do this again. It could have ripped you to pieces."

Jasper laughed. Despite the huge size, the claws and the horns, the creature was obviously docile. "It's none of your business whether I get ripped to pieces or not."

"You want to get ripped to pieces? Why don't you cross the hills and go to the dragon valley then?"

Dragon Valley. Humongous, acid spitting creatures. Apparently, nobody who ventured in that valley ever came back. Electric fences and flight disruptors isolated them to the valley, but it was definitely a sight Jasper wanted to see.

"Well, I do want to go to the viewport and try to get a sighting. I mean, that's what most people who come to Samitri want, isn't it?"

Leah fiddled with her hair. "Nowadays they mostly want to transport meat. Not a lot of tourists have been coming in the last few years."

"Since your father assumed."

"It's not his fault, though. The stupid dragons won't come near the viewport. And the orientation of the Peace Alliance was that Samitri should focus on cattle raising, not tourism."

"I still want to see the dragons. Why do you think I came to this planet?"

"I can take you there." Leah looked away as if surveying their surroundings. "Listen, I think I know something about you. You don't like girls, do you?"

Jasper knew what she implied, but decided to pretend he didn't. "I don't dislike them."

She looked away then looked back. "I mean romantically."

"Not at the moment, no." The girl with the pretty green eyes flashed through his mind, for some odd reason.

Maybe it was just that she was the last pretty girl he'd seen, not counting Leah, but Leah didn't count.

The girl sighed. Jasper suppressed a chuckle. Leah seemed to be interested in him. She touched him on the arm, shoulder, elbow, laughed at almost everything he said, but there was something quite mechanical, rehearsed about it, or maybe it was just that he couldn't reciprocate the interest, even if she was pretty. She was gorgeous, especially now as she revealed her golden skin in her light dress. Perhaps there could be some physical attraction, but then again, she didn't actually seem into it. If he'd wanted some fake physical action with a hot girl, he'd get a companion droid. Less hassle.

Jasper noticed she was anxious and fidgety, and said, "There's something you want to tell me."

Leah looked around again, and for the first time had a hint of vulnerability. "Would you keep a secret?"

"If it doesn't endanger anyone, sure."

She looked away. "My father asked me to seduce you."

Jasper's stomach turned. "And if I had been seduced? Would you kiss me? Would you go to bed with me?"

Leah shifted. "I'd maybe kiss you. As to the rest, I'd give you excuse after excuse just to postpone it long enough."

"Until what?"

She looked down. "Don't look at me like that. I have someone. My father is threatening his life. I promised I'd make you agree to marry me."

"Right. Cause I'm a puppet who can't distinguish

between what's fake and what's real, and I can't find girls on my own."

Leah fiddled with her hair. "Well, I am beautiful. But I wasn't putting much effort."

That was actually what annoyed Jasper the most, the way she fiddled with her hair and batted eyelashes, or maybe it was the vibe she sent, as if she thought she was too hot for him. Maybe she thought that just because he was albino nobody looked at him, which was completely ridiculous. But that was far from the worst thing at the moment. "And your father wants you to sell... your body?"

Leah grimaced. "No. He thinks I'd be happy with a husband who one day will be part of the Peace Alliance. He thinks love is a volatile illusion."

"Why are you telling me this other than letting me know your father is gross?"

"He's not gross! But I need your help. Please. Just until I escape, just so my father doesn't hurt Michael. Please." Leah knelt and touched his feet.

"Get up. What do you want?"

Her eyes had tears. "Please help me make my father believe we're involved. Please. It won't cost you any effort."

No effort. Right. He'd probably have to do an insane amount of pretending in the next days, but perhaps this was his opportunity. "Under one condition."

"Which condition?"

"Take me to the dragons. I don't mean the viewport. Closer."

Leah was silent for a while, then said, "Sure. I'll figure

out a way, but just close enough for you to see them. If I get you killed, my father won't be happy either."

That wasn't very promising, but at least he was getting something, and truth be told, he pitied the girl. Helping her wouldn't kill him. "Deal."

———

ALANA WALKED QUIETLY through the streets of Samitri as the sun was setting, mingling with the multitude returning from work in the farms. Her hair was tied and hidden under a hat and she wore dark-tinted glasses because she didn't want anyone memorizing her face and perhaps wondering who she was. Technically, she didn't exist in Samitri, so she'd better hide.

When she reached the market, her heart raced with memories of the previous night and her narrow escape. It also tightened with longing remembering a time long gone. The market used to be magnificent, crowded with merchants and visitors. It was reduced to nothing now, with only about one-tenth of the tents working. Her contact wasn't there, but she found Bert, the seller of souvenirs for the now almost non-existent tourists. He'd been her father's closest friend and was one of the few people who knew who she was. He also tended to be well informed.

Alana greeted him, then looked around to check if nobody was close by and said, "I saw a new guard at the port last night, very light blond hair, almost white. Any idea who that might be?"

"The albino boy? He came with the Ringon delegation. Must be security for the prince."

That didn't make sense. "I thought monarchy was over, you know, because it was awful and we're so much better now."

Bert laughed. "He's the son of someone in the Peace Alliance. They're the monarchy now, aren't they?"

"I bet they wouldn't want anyone to call their children prince."

He shrugged. "I call them whatever I want."

"As long as nobody hears it. So this guard's from Ringon." Alana tried to think whether there was any chance he'd come after her, maybe want revenge for being tased. But then, he had such kind eyes, maybe he was just a nice person in the wrong place. Who knows what job opportunities Ringon had. It's not like he'd change anything if he were to guard someone other than the pigs in the government. Alana came out of her reverie and smiled. "Thanks."

Bert had a faint laugh. "Any time."

Alana noticed how none of his dragon figures had sold in weeks. "Do you need anything to eat?"

The man looked down. Right. He was ashamed of not being able to refuse the offer.

Alana said, "Pass by our house later. You're good company. My mom will be happy."

Bert nodded. "I will."

Alana walked away wondering if the albino boy had wanted to be kind to her. Would he maybe help her escape from this planet? Oh, no. Maybe her mother had been right. She had no idea who he was and was already dreaming of escaping Samitri with him. As if he even wanted it. But she'd like to know someone from Ringon, despite their ties to the dirty Peace Alliance.

She had more important things to worry though, and headed to the Blood Tavern, entering through a back door.

Selma was in the back office and fidgeted when Alana entered. "Oh, it's you."

Alana ignored the woman's odd discomfort. "Hey, how are you?"

She shook hands with the woman and passed the chip with information. Who knows how much of a cut the woman took, but it was her best option. Anyway, had it been a fortune, the woman wouldn't be hanging around a stinky tavern. Alana at least wouldn't.

The woman then said, "There's someone I want you to meet."

Alana tensed. She had never spoken to anyone in person. Her assignments were anonymous instructions in encrypted material. A middle-aged woman with thick black hair and black eyes entered the room and gestured to Alana. "Come outside for a drink."

Selma nodded as if meaning that it was all right. Alana followed the strange woman who was too well dressed for someone from Samitri, even counting government officials and farm owners. Well, she could perhaps have something to do with the illustrious visitor in the governor's palace. Alana calmed down thinking that Selma would not want to lose a source of income. In fact, if anything, this was just more business. The woman led her to another room and closed the door.

"You're the Black Mouse, right?"

Alana nodded.

The woman chuckled. "Afraid like a mouse. This is not a trap, boy, but an opportunity. My name's Mara."

Alana shook the woman's hand, glad to be called a boy. "Black Mouse."

"Indeed. And you can fit in tight spaces, right?"

"My specialty."

Mara looked at Alana up and down. "For your sake, *boy*", her ironic tone in that word didn't go unnoticed, "I hope you're as good as they say."

"I haven't said yes."

"What does it matter, when I know the answer? Have you ever been in space?"

"No."

Mara shook her head. "No issues. It'll be quick. I need something retrieved from a spaceship, a lost spaceship that has been orbiting a planet for millennia."

Alana felt queasy. "The Ghost Ship?" That was a legendary, humongous, non-human spaceship orbiting C-2, the nearest planet in their solar system. Search teams had been sent there, and legend said nobody had ever returned. It was also called the Death Ship.

"Why that face? It's just a ship. Like the ones you enter to retrieve little things."

"I've never been in an alien spaceship, madam." Hopefully she was using the correct title.

"Few people have, have they? Since the treaty of mutual ignoring, we've just pretended they don't exist. Contact was broken. Or at least that's the official story. But it's just a ship, girl, a ship with very small passages where few people fit. You're lucky to be tiny, or else I'd need to try with a child."

The woman still assumed Alana was going to say yes. No way she'd agree on a suicide mission, and she didn't care what Selma thought of that. Still, Alana asked, "What's the pay?"

Mara had a satisfied smile. "Two. Million. Samitri credits. How's that?"

Alana made an effort not to show how excited she was. She currently made just less than a thousand credits for every standard month. Two million credits would be enough for her to live in comfort for the rest of her life, to escape Samitri, to get her mother the surgery to walk again, and to be free. Freedom!

But Alana had to negotiate. "I won't be able to do much with Samitri credits. It's all controlled, you see? I'd rather Universal Credits. Four million." Her voice had been firm, the way she'd learned to negotiate her prices, even if it usually only meant one or two hundred more Samitri credits.

Mara laughed. "I think I like you. Three million Universal Credits."

Alana was still trying to hide her excitement. "Fine. But that's pointless if I don't get out alive."

The woman stared at Alana in a serious expression. "That ship has been studied. I have a diagram of its interior. It has a small passage that you can fit through. Nobody else knows about that passage; they enter through a different entrance, one with high security. That's why they never come back. That said, I'll come with you. You'll go directly to the chamber I need. If you can enter, you can get out, right? Nothing to fear."

Alana had been waiting for so long for an opportunity to break out of her cycle, to leave this planet, to be free. She couldn't say no to it when it presented itself to her like this. Dangerous, sure—but it was everything she'd always dreamed. She extended her hand. "Deal."

3

THE GHOST SHIP

Bert and his daughter Isabelle joined Alana and her mother for dinner. Isabelle was just a little younger than Alana, and they were as friends as they could be when the girl didn't really know what Alana did for a living. Sometimes it was awkward when she had to refuse to do something in the evening without being able to explain why or lie about working on a distant farm. Thankfully it was easier when Bert was there, as he helped change the subject.

Their dinner was laski intestines with potatoes. Her mother had prepared Alana's favorite stew, even adding some expensive herbs. That smell always brought her comfort and peace. Alana was happy for the company but couldn't wait for them to go home because she wanted to tell her mother the big opportunity she had. As dinner went by, though, she realized her mother would almost die with worry if she knew what Alana was going to do, so she decided to say it was a regular job. Alana herself was almost dying with worry, but she had to trust that it would work. She had to.

———

ALANA SHUDDERED as Mara led her to a small private ship in the docks, afraid she'd be discovered, but to her surprise and relief, nobody asked for documents. Inside the ship, Mara showed and explained how to use a spacesuit. Alana shivered. That meant going out into space, not only into space, but out there, which, as far as she knew, was highly dangerous. On the other hand, Mara had a suit too, and didn't strike Alana as the suicidal type. Plus, of course an alien ship abandoned for millennia wouldn't have an artificial atmosphere. Of course.

As they took off, Alana didn't even have time to contemplate the fact that she'd leave Samitri's atmosphere for the first time as she saw her city and the surrounding farms getting smaller and smaller until the blue sky was gone and her home planet was just part of a greater something in a gigantic universe with so many stars.

A chill in her stomach wasn't the right way to put it. There was a feeling of disconnection, being away from land, almost as if she would get lost in the darkness. The thin metal walls separating her from infinity didn't give her any sense of security.

Mara looked at her and chuckled. "I know. It's overwhelming."

Alana smiled and took a deep breath to calm down. If she was this nervous now, imagine when they reached the Ghost Ship? Deep breath. It was just another ship, another assignment. Just another ship, and the fact that it was floating in nothingness and she would be wearing a suit shouldn't make any difference. In a deep breath, she reminded herself to focus. Just another assignment. The time spent sitting didn't help her calm her nerves, though.

Their planet was becoming a tiny speck in the distance. After a long time, the ship approached C-2, which at first appeared as a brown dot in the distance, and then started growing. Alana realized it was too late to quit or change her mind after all this traveling. Good. At least cowardice wouldn't tempt her.

They flew towards what looked like a dark asteroid around the planet. It wasn't an asteroid, but a ship; the Ghost Ship. Alana thought she couldn't get more nervous but she'd been wrong. It didn't look like any kind of spaceship she had ever seen. Well, of course, she'd only seen human spaceships.

The Death Ship was all black, and instead of smooth, it had curves and details on its hull, so that it looked more like some sort of monster than a flying craft. Just looking at it made her hair shiver. The idea of entering it was completely irrational. This would definitely be the point where she would give up had she been in a position where she could turn around and return, but her silent and mysterious boss didn't seem to be the kind of person who'd take her back home without what she'd come for. This wasn't a free space tourism ride. The funny thing was how come there was no tourism to the Ghost Ship, considering it was as magnificent as the Samitri dragons, perhaps more. Maybe it was the cost of travel or the fact that most people feared that ship. No surprise there. Even if she'd never heard that people had died in it, she'd be terrified just to look at it. But she was tough and would go in, take whatever she had to take, and get out. Not much different than what she usually did.

There were asteroids around the alien spacecraft. Not asteroids. Alana's stomach dropped when she recognized what the forms around the Ghost Ship were: human spacecrafts, floating aimlessly around the black abandoned ship. A reminder of what happened to people who tried to venture in it.

Mara kept her cool demeanor as she approached the black spacecraft, then attached her ship to it using the clamps. Her focus was an inspiration for Alana and a reminder that the woman knew what she was doing, so this was not a suicide mission.

The woman gave Alana the space suit. Their ship was quite small, and it was hard to put it on in the small space behind the front seats. The suit was a dark grey jumper, with a helmet attachment. There was also the breathing equipment she had to put on her back. It was all very heavy and weird. To make matters worse, Alana felt naked without access to her tasers, knives, and other tools, hidden below the thick layer of the space suit. There was something terrifying about that suit and the idea of going out in space, but there was also something magnificent and exciting.

Mara's black eyes were on her as she made the last adjustments.

"It's a golden sphere," the woman said.

"What?"

"The object you need to retrieve."

Alana took a deep breath. "Right. Any idea where I can find it?"

"No idea, but it's in the first chamber. Do not try to go anywhere else, hear me?"

Right. As if Alana were dying to explore a creepy, deathly alien spacecraft. "Don't worry."

"I'm counting on you. Don't disappoint me."

"I won't."

Alana's tone was sure, but her heart wasn't. There was something odd or perhaps menacing about the woman's words. Indeed, as Alana had assumed, she would not be able to give up on her task. The way the woman stared at her, it looked as if she'd leave her in space if she didn't retrieve the golden sphere.

The tinge of regret in Alana's chest was stupid. There was no way to change her mind now. Perhaps she should have considered that going out in space with no way of returning home by her own means was extremely risky. In fact, the woman could simply leave her there and return with no consequences and with no need to pay Alana the small fortune they'd agreed. Yes, it had been a huge mistake. Alana should have asked for more guarantees, for more assurance. Unbelievable that she hadn't thought of any of that. Right now, though, the only thing she could do was enter the ship and get the object the woman wanted.

Mara smiled. "I count on that. We're attached to the passage. Go in, retrieve the sphere, and return. Pay no matter to whatever you see there, if it's not a golden sphere."

Alana swallowed. "No problem."

Despite being warm in the suit, she felt chilled to her bones at whatever it was she wasn't supposed to mind.

They stepped into the airlock. It was a very small chamber in Mara's spaceship, only big enough for the two of them. The door behind them was shut tight, and then, slowly, the door in front of them opened. Alana's feet moved up. She was floating. Not floating. Artificial gravity was gone. Now it was not the time to remember that she had never been anywhere without gravity. Her heart could perhaps open a hole in her suit, and she feared her fast breathing would deplete her of oxygen way before her time was due.

There was no emptiness, stars, or infinite space before them, which was a relief. What Alana saw was the dark hull of the Death Ship. The surface was smooth, though.

Alana turned to Mara. "Where's the opening?"

The woman shook her head. Right. She couldn't hear her. Alana pressed the communicator on her waist belt, but before she said anything, she heard Mara's voice.

"It's there. Just go through it. It's tight, but don't be afraid."

Alana stared at the smooth metal. Go through it? Was it an illusion? She reached out her gloved hand, waiting to feel nothing, but what she felt was like a spongy texture.

"Go," Mara insisted. "You can fit in the opening. It's just tight, but it won't hurt you. Communicate with me again once you find the sphere."

Right. Alana grabbed the spongy thing to pull herself forward. It was so hard to move without gravity. She pushed herself forward, thinking that she would perhaps just go through it, but then she felt a slit, through which she moved forward with great difficulty, as if she were passing through a slit in a sponge. There was no real room for her, but, since the material was soft, she pressed it, but then it pressed on her as well. For a moment Alana thought she would be squeezed to death, but instead of having these morbid thoughts, what she needed was to move forward. Eventually she would come through.

She used her arms to push her forward, but then felt something pulling her feet. Gravity. This ship had artificial gravity, but it spooked her more than anything. How can a ship that had been abandoned for so many years have artificial gravity? At least it was easier to move through that strange wall or barrier.

She came out of that spongy wall to a dark chamber and lit the flashlight strapped to her wrist. It was a circular room, bare, except for a couple spacesuits on the floor. Alana took a closer look and almost retched. They were bodies, small bodies; children. Alana almost froze, realizing that the woman waiting for her outside had tried this before. No. Maybe somebody else had brought them. The question is how come they hadn't escaped. Golden sphere, that was what she had to find, and as long as she found it, nobody would dare leave her behind.

The chamber was bare, though. Only floor, ceiling, and walls. Walls. What if they had been made with the same material as her exit? Alana looked back. Her exit was different, though, it was a lighter grey, not as dark as the rest of the wall. Perhaps Alana could find something like that. She considered talking to Mara and asking for more details but she feared that the woman would just leave her behind if she thought Alana wasn't going to bring the sphere. It was a matter of life and death now, beyond the point of regret and looking back at her recklessness and naivety.

Alana tried to calm down and looked carefully at the rest of the circular wall, trying to find some pattern, something. What she did find was what looked like another opening, on the opposite side from where she'd come. It had the same grey color but was much bigger. That said, if it was a door, it would lead her to other chambers, exactly what Mara had asked her not to do. Even if the woman had no scruples, she certainly wanted the sphere, thus it was better to heed her instructions and not cross that wall.

Alana examined the wall again, this time looking at the floor, and with difficulty noticed that there were small grey circles on its bottom. Or was she imagining things? She knelt and touched one of those circles. That spongy texture. She touched the wall around it; it was hard. Right. So the circles were openings. In theory, she could check each circle, but she had a feeling she'd better try to get it right at once. How could she figure out alien logic, though? Well, the chamber had two doors, one opposite the other.

If someone had wanted to put the sphere in an obvious position, they'd choose the middle. If they had wanted to hide it, they'd choose somewhere else. Would they need to hide it, though? In their own ship? Alana moved to one of the circles between the two doors and stuck her arm inside it. It was tight and deep, but it didn't discourage her. When she had her arm way past the elbow in, she felt something. It wasn't round, though, but pointy. It could be a part of the hull, and then it could also be some special object. Alana decided to leave it alone and moved to the other side.

In the opposite middle circle, after she'd stuck her arm, she found something, but it felt like a cube. Alana was tempted to take it, to bring home more treasures, but, again, a sense of dread made her hesitate. All right. So the sphere wasn't in the middle, and her next option was to check the other circles. Indeed each of them had some kind of object, but they were easily identifiable as not spheric. Alana's priority was to survive, and for that, she'd need the prized object the woman wanted. With that, she could barter for her life—and hopefully something more.

Maybe she should contact Mara and let her know that it wouldn't take much longer, as she feared that the woman would grow impatient and take off. No. The order was to contact her only once she had the sphere, and that was what she was going to do. Alana kept checking, and had checked about a third of the circles in that chamber. Her elbow was sore from stretching, and her arm hurt from being squeezed in those tight spongy openings. Her only consolation was that at least she was finding things in those openings, and, by logic, she would find the sphere as well.

Another circle. This time, Alana touched something smooth and round. Round on all sides; a sphere. With much difficulty, she pulled it, and had the greatest relief sigh she'd had in her entire life. She would be saved and come home. Alana examined the object. It was just a smooth golden sphere. Strange. She'd thought that it either contained something inside or was some kind of equipment, but it didn't appear so. Perhaps its material was precious. Right then, she felt a rumbling sound, as if the Alien ship had been a stomach growling in hunger. Who knew what equipment still worked in it? Either way, she wouldn't know, as she was leaving.

Alana touched her communicator. "I have it. I'm coming."

Silence on the other end.

Alana tried again. "Are you there?" Her voice was shaky.

"Yes. Yes," the woman replied, as if coming back from a long reverie. "I'll open the airlock for you."

Alana walked to the opening from where she'd entered the ship. This time, it seemed harder to go through. Perhaps she was just tired. The wall felt tighter to the point it hurt her body. She feared being squeezed alive, but perhaps it was nonsense. She'd come in, right? But it was almost impossible to move forward. Alana moved some more and felt hard wall in front of her. This couldn't be. She was in the right place, she knew it!

A hand stretched out in front of her. "Give it to me," Mara's voice sounded in her ear.

"I need to get out."

"Give it to me and I'll help you get out."

No way. If Alana let go of the sphere, she'd have nothing. "Help me get out and I'll give it to you."

"Don't be silly," Mara insisted. "I can help you, but I need to make sure I have what I need."

"Help me get out and you'll find out."

"Girl, if you don't give it to me, I'll have to leave you. Don't think keeping the sphere will save you. I can just leave you and send someone else to retrieve it."

"I can hide it, madam. And I'll make sure I hide it so well that nobody will be able to find it. So what do you say? Help me?" The wall was pressing Alana back inside, but she grabbed the woman's hand. "Pull me, please?"

"The sphere, the sphere!" The woman was screaming.

Alana clutched the hand, and it was harder and harder to hold on to it, as the wall pressed her backwards.

A horrible scream echoed in her communicator. "Let go!"

Alana was pulled back inside the chamber while still holding on to the woman. No, she was holding the hand and arm, and wanted to scream in horror at the pool of blood forming in front of her. Mara was no longer attached to the arm, which had been ripped from her.

A horrible voice sounded. "Stupid little girl! You'll die there, and I hope you die in pain!"

The communicator was turned off. Alana's flashlight also stopped working. She hadn't guessed that it could be controlled remotely. In the dark, alone with a severed arm and a precious golden sphere, with no way to return to her planet, Alana understood that it was her end. For so long she had wanted to break through, to escape her confinement and poverty. In a way, she was escaping.

4

INFINITY

Mistakes could be corrected in land. In space, a mistake was certain death. Alana should have considered that. She sat down, thinking about the children who'd come before her, if they had been scared, or what they had felt when left alone. Better not to think about it. Her heart was tight thinking about her mother. Would she even guess what had happened? Would anyone know? It hurt her to think about her mother having to live with the uncertainty whether Alana was dead, alive, enslaved, suffering... Her mother didn't deserve that and didn't deserve to live without Alana there to help her either. Such a stupid mistake. It should have been obvious from the start that going into space with a stranger was not a good idea. But dazzled with the promise of a fortune, Alana had chosen to ignore everything. Now she wouldn't have either a fortune or even her life.

Her eyes were getting used to the dark and she could see the shapes where the bodies were. Dark. But there had to be some light, even if just a little, or else she wouldn't see a thing. Alana lifted the sphere in front of her eyes. It had a strange gold glow. In its middle, a glowing line and some writing in an Alien, forgotten language. The line looked like a groove, and of course she wouldn't have felt it with her thick gloves. It made sense that this wouldn't be a solid sphere; it was just a container. At this point, opening a valuable object wouldn't help Alana's life much, but maybe it was curiosity, or maybe just a petty desire to ruin whatever was inside it so as to prevent Mara from getting it.

Alana twisted top and bottom in opposite directions, to see if she could open it by twisting, but nothing happened. Her gloves made everything difficult, though. Alana could perhaps remove her gloves just long enough to twist or try to open the sphere. She wouldn't lose her hands in a couple seconds, and then, what would a dead body need hands for? Alana held the golden ball between her knees and removed the gloves.

There was no normal cold or even freaky deathly space cold. Well, the spaceship had gravity. Was it that much of a stretch that it kept its inner temperature inside at tolerable levels? Now that she touched the sphere with her hands, she could feel the groove. At first she twisted it with no results, then she tried to simply pull the pieces apart using her nails to try to break it, then finally tried to mix pulling apart and twisting. It didn't open. She finally tried to press them together. At that, the sphere didn't open, but a strong ray of light came out of it, directed upwards. Alana looked away, turning back slowly when she felt her eyes were adjusted.

There was a column of light, and, in the middle of it, a tiny humanoid figure; a blue woman in a loose black dress with dark blue hair and what looked like some horns. Maybe Alana was dying and hallucinating, maybe it was the lack of oxygen, which by the way, she'd never asked how long would last. The little woman gestured as if she were removing an imaginary helmet. Right. That suggestion was for Alana. Her still ungloved hands told her that the temperature inside the ship was bearable, but she feared being without oxygen. Well, that was stupid, as her breathing equipment was a mask, and not the helmet. Alana unclamped her helmet. It had a fasten and hung from her neck.

The figure inside the light seemed eager to say something, but Alana spoke first. "What are you?"

The little woman looked down at herself and back to Alana, and chucked. "What? Don't you mean who? Or am I an object to you?"

"That's what I'm asking."

The little woman shook her head. "No, no, no. See? You ruined my presentation. I had all this speech prepared and perfected during my time of confinement." She looked at Alana. "Nine hundred ninety-nine years... Your years." She chuckled. "Funny you should count time based on how long a long-dead planet used to turn around its star, but that's it. Nine hundred ninety-nine years I've been here, and I had this presentation planned, but I wasn't waiting for someone asking me what I was."

Alana was startled and somewhat amused. "Do your presentation, then. If you take too long I might die, so you won't get to do it any time soon." Maybe it could be soon, if Mara sent someone else, but she didn't want to think about that.

The small woman took a deep breath, then said, "You have awoken me from a three-thousand cycle sleep, and, uh—"

"Something wrong?"

"I'm getting stressed."

Right. "Just answer my questions, then. Who are you, and why are you in this thing? Are you in this sphere, or is this a hologram?"

"My name is one you should give me. I am both here and not here, but I'm at your service."

"Right. Wow, thanks. At my service. That's exactly what I need." She didn't want to be rude to the little woman, but the irony of having someone in her service when facing death was hard to ignore. "Can you get me back to Samitri?"

"Is that your first wish?"

"Probably my last, but that's not a problem now, is it?"

The little woman stared at her. "Last?" She laughed. "You think you're going to die! You're not going to die. Not with me here. See, I can help you get what you want."

Alana was doubtful. "Like returning to Samitri?"

"Yes."

She still thought it was a bunch of nonsense, but she wanted to test how far it went. "What about after I return? Could you help me get to Ringon? Find a way to make a fortune?"

"Yes, yes. That's why I had to do the presentation. See, since you found and opened me, I'll help you achieve what you want."

It sounded far fetched. "Anything I want? Isn't there a limit or something?"

The little woman considered her. "Well, a limit... Yes, you can wish for three things only."

"And you said you could get me back to Samitri."

"For sure. Is that your first wish?"

Alana tried to think. Even on the brink of death, her negotiation instinct kicked in. Three was not a lot. There was a high possibility that this little woman in the sphere wouldn't be able to do anything, but then, Mara wanted something, so maybe, maybe it was true. If it was true, Alana didn't want to waste a wish just getting back home.

She said, "Getting back to Samitri is important so that I survive. If I die, I can't make any wishes, so I don't think it counts. It's more like a prerequisite for the three wishes, if you know what I mean."

The little woman considered her. "I'm not sure."

"And I need to know if you can really do what you say you can, right? I mean, for all I know you could be some kind of prank planted here by your... Who set you up?"

The woman looked away. "I cannot tell you that, but it wasn't you humans. I'm not a prank, but I'll get you back to your planet as a sign of good will. You need to name me, though."

"Name you? Like what? Is there a name you want?"

"You choose the name. It's how you can call me."

"Janet. Do you like Janet?"

"Janet works."

"Right. Janet, so you said you can get me back to my planet, right?" Alana almost scoffed at the ridiculousness of believing in that, but she absolutely had nothing to lose.

"Yes, but you'll need to trust me."

Alana shrugged. "It's not like I have better plans of my own, you know?"

Janet had a light chuckle. "No. I mean, really trust me. If you stray away from my direction, it won't work, and it won't be my fault."

"Like I said, I have no plans of my own. So what do I need to do to get back home?"

"Back to your planet, you said."

"To my planet."

"There's another piece that goes with this, and you'll have to retrieve it."

"Sure thing. Where is it?" Following this conversation relieved Alana from her fear of death and her worries about her mother.

"The other side of the ship."

Alana remembered Mara telling her not to go anywhere. "Isn't it dangerous going there?"

"There's always danger. But I'll help you."

Well, the alternative was sitting and waiting for death to

come and get her. Perhaps it would be better to speed up the process.

Janet pointed to the opening opposite the one Alana had come from. "You have to go through there."

Insane. Totally insane. Alana walked towards the big grey circle.

Janet said, "Wait. It closes and opens, you see? If you don't go at the right moment you could be crushed to death inside the wall."

"How do I know when I can go through?"

"You don't. But I do. Wait."

Alana wasn't in a hurry anyway and waited what must have been a few minutes, thinking about running out of oxygen, running out of time, running out of life, while following a mini hologram for a plan that sounded ludicrous.

"Now!" Janet said.

Alana crossed the spongy opening, still feeling her body being squeezed, but able to move forward. After she crossed it, once she noticed where she was, her heart almost stopped. She was at a ledge bordering the most gigantic chamber she had ever seen. So much empty space beneath and above her, and nothing in front of her. Suddenly she hated that artificial gravity. Thanks to it, if she fell it would be certain death.

"You can't fly, right?" Janet asked.

"No." What kind of question was that?

"Hum, it's tricky then." She pointed to another ledge at a few meters from where Alana was, with nothing but wall between them. "You'll need to hold on to the wall and move there."

At this point, the mission looked like suicide. "I might fall."

"There's enough room for a human like you to hold, and your arms are just strong enough. You won't fall. This won't work if you don't trust me."

Fine. Alana turned around, looking for a groove, a hook, something, but all she noticed was that the wall was rough. Hardly rough enough for her to move through it.

Janet said. "It's easier far from the ledge. You'll find places to put your hands and feet."

Right. Alana put the sphere in her huge front pocket, which must have been designed to carry stuff like that, then went to the edge, and reached out her hand and leg, until she did find a small hole for one of her feet and another for one of her hands. She then found something not as great for the other foot and hand, but she kept moving into the abyss without looking down. Slowly she moved sideways until she reached the other ledge. She could barely believe she'd made it, and at this point was getting very worried about oxygen, since her breathing had been fast due to the effort and fear. She took the sphere and faced the little woman.

"What now?"

"See that plug?" Janet pointed to a small hole on the bottom of the wall. "Insert me there."

"How?"

"As if you were sticking me into it. Get me out once the artificial gravity is off."

Alana was going to say that the size didn't fit, but then she decided she'd waste less time just trying what she'd been told, so she turned the sphere and put it in the hole. She heard a click and assumed whatever she'd done was correct.

Again she waited, and again she had time to wonder at the insanity of all that was happening. But then, even if she had one chance in one million to survive, she'd grab it; one remote possibility of going back home, back to her mother. She felt a chill in her stomach. No, not a chill, it was as if it was light, and then her feet were no longer touching the ledge. Gravity was gone. Alana pulled back the sphere.

"What now?"

"You need to move across the chamber, but quickly, as the gravity will return in thirty seconds."

"Thirty—" Damn it, it was no time to complain. "How do I go across?"

"Push yourself against the wall. Put all your strength. Quickly."

Alana pressed her feet on the wall. She wanted to bend her legs and do as if she were jumping, but she couldn't get too close, so she did the best she could, and indeed started moving across the abyss, even if a lot slower than she would have liked.

Janet said, "It should have been stronger."

"Why?" Alana tried to suppress the panic. She was beyond panic. "You think I won't make it?"

"You'll barely make it. You should put me in your pocket, as you'll need your arms."

Neat. Janet put the sphere in her front pocket and closed it. But Janet was likely wrong because Alana was getting to the ledge on the opposite side where there was a door. Getting was the word here, as she began to fall and had to hold on the ledge. With a lot of effort, she pushed herself up, then took the sphere and said, "How many times am I going to almost die before I get to my planet?"

"Almost is a meaningless concept. What I can say is that if you trust me you won't die before reaching your planet."

"So what do I do now?"

"Go through the door."

This was not like the spongy surface, but a metal circle.

Janet said, "The button beside it."

Alana pressed it, and the door opened, leading to a very long hallway with transparent windows from where she could see the universe around her.

Alana risked a question. "Why do people die on this ship?"

"They don't understand it."

"But you do."

"Yes, I do."

"So you think I'll get out alive?"

"If you do what I say."

Right. Alana would have to trust a mini hologram in a strange object. Not like she had any other choice. They went to the end of the hallway, then through another circular door to smaller hallways and smaller chambers, until they found something looking like a control room, with six walls, each with a panel in it, except for the wall with the door.

Allana had a question. "How come there are no bodies here?"

"People rarely come that far."

"How can you know it, if you've been in this sphere for —you said almost a thousand years, right?"

"I wasn't in it. I'm contained in it, but had I been in it, I would never be able to help you achieve anything. What can I know from inside a sphere? I'm not my container."

Alana wasn't sure she understood, but this wasn't a good time to debate it. "I see."

"Now you're going to press exactly what I tell you."

"Can't you do the plug thing again?"

"Not this time."

Alana obeyed, touching panels she'd never seen before, not knowing exactly what she was doing or for what. Well, maybe knowing a little couldn't hurt. "Why am I doing this?"

"To tell the ship to let you out."

"*Tell* the ship? You say it as if it were alive or something."

"It has a consciousness."

"And it murders people."

"Intruders. And it's not on purpose."

"Do *you* have a consciousness?"

"For sure. I'm alive, you see?"

No. Alana didn't see it, but she accepted it, or perhaps

just pretended she did. After this level, they went to another chamber, just like the first one.

Janet said, "Now you'll have to take the small sphere from the third opening on the right of the door."

Alana again had to stretch her arm to get it. It was a small golden sphere, similar to the one where Janet was. "What is this?"

"Put it in your ear."

Alana did it.

Janet's voice came from the small sphere. "Can you hear me?"

"Yes."

"Good. You can now put your helmet. You can still talk to me. I'll hear you anywhere. But you'll need to use this to hear me. You can put the big sphere in your suit pocket. What we're going to do now is very precise, so you'll need to listen to everything carefully. If you're not sure of what I'm telling you, ask for clarifications. Is that clear?"

"Yes." Alana attached the helmet, glad that she'd no longer need to carry that bulky thing with her.

"Now comes the hard part." Janet's voice came from the small sphere in Alana's ear.

Hard part? After she had almost fallen? And plus she couldn't imagine how she'd go back to her planet when she didn't have a spacecraft and when she didn't know how to pilot. She hadn't asked anything about it because perhaps not knowing would keep her hopeful. Maybe.

Following Janet's instructions, Alana walked back to the big empty chamber and climbed up on it. She made an effort to keep her feet steady and her heart from speeding up too much. She didn't look down and tried to tell herself this was just a game, that this wasn't a death-deep chamber, just climbing up to get to a hard-to-reach place in a ship in Samitri's port. She missed that port, missed everything about her planet, and, most of all, missed her mother. She also wished she could have spoken with the blond guard who had spared her. She'd never thanked him, and only now realized how, for once in her life, she'd had someone do an act of kindness for her without gaining anything in return and without even knowing her.

They came to a platform near the ceiling of the huge chamber.

At this point, Alana was doubting whatever Janet had in stock for her. "You do realize I need a spaceship to go back home, right? I mean, why am I here?"

"To solve your problem. Your oxygen won't last long. We'll waste a lot of time if I have to explain everything. But the idea is obviously to get a ship."

This was an odd place for a hangar, but then, wasn't everything about that spaceship odd? They came to stairs leading to a trapdoor.

"You need to go up here."

Alana followed and entered a small chamber. It looked very much like an airlock, except it couldn't be. If Janet was leading her to a place where she could find a ship, it obviously couldn't be in outer space.

Janet said, "Make sure your helmet and gloves are well attached."

There was something worrisome about these instructions, but Alana just did as she'd been told. There was another circular door with a button by its side.

Janet said pointed to a bar on the wall. "Hold on to it, and then press the button."

Alana obeyed and her heart almost stopped. What lay in front of her was the infinite universe, with many more stars than she could possibly count. Without gravity, Alana was floating, being held to the ship by holding onto the bar.

"Is this some joke?" Alana's voice was shaky.

"I told you to trust me," Janet replied. "Where do you think you'll find a ship?"

"In an inner hangar! Don't you have an inner hangar?"

"Not on this ship. Now, I'm serious, if you want to go back to your planet, you'll have to start trusting me. Any mistake, any misstep, any hesitation could cost your life, and it won't be my fault."

"That's so comforting. What if you're wrong? What if you're lying?"

"You can go back and wait for someone to rescue you, except nobody will come."

Again, Alana remembered Mara's interest in that sphere. Would that woman be willing to kill someone just to get hold of a pranky object? Unlikely. Surrender, trust, relax. Could she do it? It was her one shot, her one chance, and even if she thought that chance was not really true, she had no alternative.

Alana took a deep breath. "I'll do whatever you say."

"Good. As you noticed, there are ships orbiting this

spacecraft. It's a form of magnetism. You'll get in one of those, one that has fuel and still works."

"How?" Her voice had come out more annoyed and incredulous than she'd intended. "I mean, what am I supposed to do?"

"Wait. When the right time comes, you have to push yourself in that direction. Push yourself against the hull of this ship, in the right angle, and it should work."

Should. But then, perhaps if it didn't work, it would be better to die trying. Maybe it would be good to die floating in space as if she were a tiny star. Then, maybe, it was better not to think about dying.

Janet said, "On your guard. I can say now at any moment."

Alana had trouble breathing, and it wasn't that her air was gone yet. With her heart at that rate, she was probably burning through the oxygen way faster than she should. There were indeed a few crafts surrounding the Ghost Ship, but none of them close enough that she would be able to reach them.

Janet said, "Do you see that star in that cluster? The one that's a bit pink?"

"Yes."

"Wait until I tell you so, but you'll go in that direction."

"There's nothing there."

"There will be."

Alana's heartbeat reverberated through her body, her suit, and her helmet as she waited for the command.

"Now!" Janet said.

Surrender. Trust. Listen.

Alana pushed her legs against the hull and moved in that direction, even though she didn't see any ship where she was going. Her movement was towards the void of space, floating aimlessly.

If Janet made a mistake, Alana would have no means to return to the Ghost Ship or even try to go anywhere else, since she would no longer be able to find something to push against. That said, she moved faster than she'd expected, likely due to the absence of resistance.

Had Alana been sure that she'd come out of this alive, she'd be able to enjoy this experience, enjoy flying in space with nothing around her but her thin suit, despite how terrifying it was. Maybe the reason she would enjoy it was the fact that it was terrifying but exhilarating at the same time. How many people had ever jumped in space towards nothing? She just hoped she could live to remember this experience.

But then, wasn't life a great jump in the dark from which nobody came out alive? Getting philosophical wasn't a good sign. She wanted to ask Janet something, double check that the miniature woman hadn't made a mistake, but then, she feared what answer she was going to get.

Far away, she saw something that looked like a small spacecraft, but it wasn't exactly in front of her, but rather to her left. "Am I in the right direction?"

"Yes. And yes, that's the spaceship we're aiming for."

Alana couldn't bottle down the panic taking hold of her. "But I'm not going in its direction!"

"Of course not. If you go towards the direction where it is now, you'll never reach it. You need to go where it's going."

Hopefully that was what she was doing, or else she would indeed die floating in the universe. But then, her oxygen would eventually deplete. Did it really make any difference whether she was inside a ship or floating outside? No. The best scenario would be grabbing that ship, though. As she moved, however, she noticed that she was approaching that craft, or else it was approaching her trajectory, and started to believe that she had a shot at survival.

"You can move," Janet said. "Tilt towards the ship."

Alana bent her body, and her movement continued towards the silver ship, realizing she was moving faster than she'd thought at first and that the ship wasn't exactly in front of her.

"Stretch and grab it!" Janet yelled.

Alana threw her body to the side and stretched her arm as much as she could until she grabbed a cable coming from that ship. Her oxygen would definitely finish before it was due, the way she was breathing.

"See?" Janet said. "It wasn't hard."

Not hard at all except that if Alana had missed the cable she'd be now floating aimlessly without hope of finding anything.

Janet continued, "I chose this ship because it had cables and it has handles on the outside, for EVA. It still has enough fuel. Move towards the top part and you'll find an airlock."

Alana could move easily now by pulling the cable. She was attentive not to let it go, though. On the top, she found a trapdoor, and, with Janet's instructions, entered the empty ship. It had no lights, and she stumbled on a seat before taking the sphere and getting Janet out. It was a light, after all.

"I assume you're going to tell me how to get this thing on."

Janet chuckled. "What do you think? Would all that effort have been for nothing?"

"A lot of effort is for nothing."

"Indeed. But not from us. Go to the front. There. Yes. There's a panel. I'll tell you what to do."

"How did you even know this was open, how can you even pilot it? Do you have some kind of universal pilot training in your planet?"

"Not planet training, Alana. Just cosmic knowledge."

"And the cosmos knows how to pilot all kinds of ships?"

"Ships are built by humans, aren't they? Connected to the infinite consciousness."

"Yeah, yeah. Just tell me what to do."

Janet was back to her straightforward instructions, and Alana followed, touching strange buttons. Now, Alana didn't know much about piloting other than the basic notions she had to have as someone who often went in and out of ships. That said, she had never seen anything like this.

"Is this ship Alien?"

"It's human, but, for your kind, it's considered old. That's why it looks strange to you."

"I see."

"Humans have a need to change things up so that perfectly functioning machines will be obsolete."

"So they buy new ones. People like new stuff—when we can buy them."

"And that's the issue, isn't it? Now you'll have to be very careful. A tiny mistake could send you to the wrong coordinates, and then you won't have either air or fuel to find your way back."

"No pressure."

"You find your attitude amusing. Interesting. Right. Enter the number 085565 on the right panel." Alana did as she'd been told. "Right. Now you'll push the main lever."

Alana didn't see anything. "Where?"

"On your left, in the bottom."

Alana would have called it a switch, but then maybe there was an issue of scale going on there. Alana pushed it —and felt the ship move. "What do I have to do now?"

"Nothing. It's on auto-pilot."

"So I cross my arms and wait to get home?"

"To your planet. You wouldn't want to land in your house, would you?"

"Figure of speech."

"Careful with those figures," Janet said. "I could misunderstand them."

"But we're going to Samitri, right?"

"That's what you wanted."

Alana felt something odd. A weird mix of relief with disbelief and even some fear. But the ship was moving, and after some time she saw her planet. It should be a familiar sight of home, except that she'd never seen it from space. Pictures and videos didn't compare to the feeling of seeing that tiny ball grow bigger and bigger.

For the first time, Alana thought that she was going to survive this, and it was weird to realize that, until then, she'd given herself up for dead. Now that she realized she would maybe survive, the notion that she possessed a strange, powerful object or being dawned on her.

Alana marveled at the idea of wishing for anything she wanted. Her first thought was that she should ask for help to leave Samitri with her mother and to get her mother the surgery. Those were two requests right there, out of three. What next? She had to think well before deciding on anything, and had to be strategic. Well, that is if she really landed.

Her planet was now the biggest thing on her view as if about to swallow her. Only then, Alana considered the logistics of what she was doing. "Will they allow me to land? At the port?"

"You're not going there."

"What?"

5
<hr>

VALLEY

Jasper had been taken to a location far from the dragon viewports.

Leah leaned over a fence. "I've heard that some photographers used to come here. In theory, it should allow you to get a better look."

Still, behind the fence, staring at the gigantic valley below him, Jasper wasn't sure if he'd see anything. The towers with flight interrupting frequencies were probably scaring away the dragons and maybe even hurting their natural patterns. No wonder the animals were dangerous. Jasper wondered if too much precaution had caused the dragons to be more aggressive than they'd normally be. He'd studied a little of the history of Samitri and the dragons, and heard that there had been very few attacks before the valley had been isolated. After its isolation, when anyone ventured into it, the result had been instant death.

Even so, Jasper wanted to go in. With his knowledge, experience with wild creatures, and his extensive reading on Samitri dragons, he had great survival chances. The issue was either convincing Leah to let him get in, or else distracting her long enough for her not to freak out and ruin his chances. His odds would be zero if he went in and she kept yelling his name in desperation.

Still, from that distance, he tried to get a sight from his binoculars. Nothing. If they'd been extinct it would be a sad loss to add to humanity's heinous crimes. When people wondered why he preferred wild creatures, that was the answer. No killing for no reason, for money, for greed.

As he watched, he finally saw something different happening. A meteor. No, not a meteor, a spaceship. Someone was crashing in the dragon valley. This could maybe be his opportunity for a better sighting. If dragons were really attracted by humans, and if there was someone inside the ship, they would come for them. For a moment he almost had a cruel pleasure in imagining what could happen. But no, perhaps whoever was inside it had no blame at all, in that odd way humans claimed no blame for what their ancestors and their species did. It was far from where he was, but still close enough to the towers that the dragons perhaps wouldn't approach. But then, close enough to the towers that they would be extremely irritable and dangerous.

"What's that?" Leah's voice interrupted his thoughts.

"A ship crashed."

"I'll call for help."

Calling for help could be worse. "Leah, listen, please. Don't call anyone. They might bring hovers, they'll do things that will just make the dragons more aggressive. I'll go in. Do not, no matter what happens, do not scream or yell my name."

"I can't let you do that."

Jasper pointed to the craft. "Then whoever's there might die. I'm going in. If you call for help or if you yell you'll be responsible for two deaths."

He moved towards the electric fence, meaning to climb it.

"It's electrified!" Leah warned.

"I'll deal with it."

Jasper had come prepared and used an electricity disruptor. It would break the current for just a few seconds. Leah watched in silence, perhaps too shocked or stunned to say anything or yell, which was a good sign. The girl obviously didn't care if he lived or died but cared about what her father would think if he got killed. Charming friend.

He jumped inside and turned to see Leah staring at him, her face pale. Oh, well. So far so good. He walked slowly towards the ship, eyes alert. Maybe whoever was inside was already dead, but then, maybe not. Five minutes before he'd been telling himself he preferred animals to people, and how he was doing this. Why? Maybe it was just another dangerous rescue operation, and perhaps it was more about the danger than about helping. No, that wasn't true. He did like to help.

As he approached the ship, he noticed that it was an ancient model, and wondered who would still be using that. Perhaps pirates or someone in a desperate escape. It could be someone dangerous in there. He had a taser gun, and that was all, but then, he doubted whoever was there would attack the person trying to help them.

To his surprise and relief, the spacecraft could be opened from the outside. He entered it and saw that there was a person in the pilot seat struggling to get out. He approached—and was stunned. It was the girl who'd been hiding in the box at the market, the girl who'd been running away. Now, what was she doing coming from space in a century-old ship?

"You."

The girl tensed. Funny how he knew that look.

He continued, "I'm here to help. You're in the Dragon Valley."

"I know." There was a hinge of offense in her voice. "What are you doing here?"

Jasper snorted. "Me? I'm not the one coming from outer space. You do know that this planet has a port, right?"

The girl rolled her eyes. "I'll be sure to crash there next time."

"No, now I'm serious. You know that the dragons out there, they could kill you, right?"

"Really? I was thinking of adopting one as a pet."

Jasper ignored her sarcasm. "I can help you get out, but you'll need to do as I say."

"Why?"

"I spent four years in the forests of Faris rescuing and taking care of wild creatures. I've read all about the Samitri dragons. I know how to deal with them, and I can help you get out of this valley in one piece."

The girl stared at him, then sighed. "Well, first of all, I need to get unstuck, or nothing is going to happen."

"Let me see." He approached her. The seat restraint had been broken in the crash, and now was stuck and wouldn't come up. "Don't move."

"As if I could."

Jasper smiled, punched the bar sideways, paying a lot of attention not to hit her, and then kicked the lever on the bottom. The restraint snapped out of place.

The girl sighed in relief. "Thank you."

"Thank me once we're out of this valley." He extended his hand. "I'm Jasper."

The girl looked down. "I can't. I can't tell you my name."

"No problem, mysterious girl. You can still shake my hand, though."

The girl looked at him, an odd expression as if examining him, and then shook his hand. She was visibly scared, and it wasn't of the dragons. Well, nobody would avoid saying their names in fear of reptiles—or at least he hoped so.

He tried to calm her, "I won't harm you."

The girl frowned. "That's not what I thought."

"Good."

He gave her what he thought was a reassuring smile. Her mouth had a slight smile in return, so it must have worked. Her eyes didn't move away from him, though. This was one annoying thing in dealing with humans. He could never tell whether they were staring because they wanted to understand why his skin was so fair, if it was because it was the first albino they saw, or if it was for some other reason.

Her green eyes were pretty, though, and he looked away once he realized he had been staring back. The girl was wearing a suit for extravehicular activity. That was intriguing, but he wasn't going to ask because she was probably not going to answer, and the priority now was to get her to safety.

He said, "All right. I didn't see any dragons, but once we get out, we need to be on the lookout. No matter what happens, don't run. I mean it, and it might be hard because you'll have to fight your instincts. Do not run."

"Right."

"Don't smile at them."

The girl had a grimace. "You think I'd want to charm them?"

Jasper shrugged. "I'm just saying. They could think you're baring your teeth. Don't scream, don't yell, and don't turn your back to them."

She nodded. "Fine. Wait. What if they encircle us? How can I not give them my back?"

That was quite unlikely, as it wasn't their hunting pattern. Either way, humans were not the food they ate. If anything, they would be looking only into defending themselves or getting rid of intruders. Still, he said, "We can stand back-to-back."

She nodded. "That makes sense."

"Last thing, don't look directly in their eyes. They could think it's a challenge."

"I won't."

He looked around. "I think you'll lose your ship, though. It won't be safe to return and try to get it going."

She looked around and shrugged. "It's not my ship."

He wondered if she'd stolen it, then felt bad for that assumption. He decided to ask, "How did you get it? Do you need to return it?"

She had a playful smile. "I found it floating in space."

"Of course."

Jasper could have told her that either she answered his questions or he would leave her in the valley, but he didn't want to press her. Plus, at the bottom of it all was just fear. It wasn't that strange to be feared, even if it felt uncomfortable now.

He climbed to the top and extended his hand. "Come."

Again she had a tiny smile, then took his hand as he helped her up. She stared at him again, but looked away when their eyes met. Perhaps he'd also been staring.

They climbed down the hull. The girl landed gracefully beside him on the ground. Still no sounds of dragons, even though they were far enough from the towers that it would be possible for the creatures to approach. Maybe the crash had scared them. If that was really the case, that would be new information he'd like to note. He was going to head back to the gate where Leah was, but then he turned to the girl. "You're hiding your identity, right?"

She halted, eyes wide. "I never said that."

"That's not the kind of stuff you say, though. But tell me, would it be a problem if a Samitri governor saw you? If they knew where you'd come from?"

The girl swallowed and stared as if planning what to say.

Jasper spared her the need to come up with an acceptable excuse. "I get it. I'll take you to a different exit, where there won't be anyone—I think. Is that good for you?"

She nodded, her head movement a little too fast. If only he could convince her that she would never have any reason to fear him... Maybe she just needed time.

There was another disrupting tower to their right. It would be about a thirty-minute walk, but he wasn't sure if he wanted to go back to where Leah was. Even if she was nice and friendly, she was still the governor's daughter, and could maybe compromise the Mysterious Girl. He just hoped the dragons didn't make their exit difficult. Still, so far there had been no signs of any of them, and maybe the trend would continue.

They had walked a while when she broke the silence. "Why are you helping me?"

"Have you ever considered that it's weird that people need reasons to help each other?"

"No. That said, no person can help everyone, nobody has that much reach. It means you'll need to pick who you help. So the choice matters."

Jasper nodded. "True. I was here, watching the valley, and I saw a ship crash. I thought doing something was within my reach. Same thing that night, when the guards were chasing you. I saw you, I knew you were scared, I could do something, and I did it. Maybe it's just a matter of taking the opportunities."

She was thoughtful. "Coincidence."

"True. Twice I see you now. Twice you won't tell me who you are. I just hope you don't tase me this time."

"I will if I have to."

"You won't have to."

She smiled. He still wanted to ask her name, but he thought that she'd feel more at ease if he respected her privacy and her limits.

"You're from Ringon, aren't you?" she asked.

"I was born there. Last years of my life were spent on Faris."

She seemed puzzled.

He added, "The jungle planet."

"Do people live there?"

"Not a lot. I did. I liked it and I miss it."

"Why are you here then?"

"The same reason people used to come to this planet many years ago." He jerked his head to the middle of the valley. "Dragons." That was just part of the truth, but he didn't want to mention his mother's wish for him to come.

"Apparently they've become shy lately."

"Something's happening, and that's what I want to find out."

"Don't you have to work?"

An odd question. Maybe not. As the Peace Alliance official, he was there in a supervisory capacity. "Maybe it's part of my work, right? Checking things. And you? Don't you have to work?"

She looked away and seemed upset.

"Sorry," Jasper said. "I didn't mean—"

She stared at him, but this was a completely different kind of stare, with hard eyes. "Everybody in Samitri works, and you know that. Or at least you should."

Jasper felt like a fool, and he'd give anything to have her stare at him like she'd been doing before. "I'm not inquiring on that. I swear. I'm not from here. I'm trying to protect you."

"Don't ask those questions, then."

"You haven't even told me your name, and I'm here taking a longer way to get out of the valley, just so you aren't recognized. You should consider that."

"Sorry. I just—"

"It's fine." He realized then he hadn't been listening for dragons and looked around to see if there were any creatures near them. "We should keep our voices down."

"I know," she whispered.

She didn't seem nervous, though, or at least not quite as afraid as she should be. Perhaps she had no idea what the dragons could do, or perhaps it had been so long that they hadn't shown up that she just didn't believe she would see them. In fact, he was starting to think the same, wondering if the dragons were some kind of hoax to cover up for something or worse, if they had been extinct. Jasper would be very pissed if that had been the case.

Just then, he heard a sound that froze his bones. As far as it was, and as much as it was a sound he'd never heard before, he recognized the pain and fear in it. There was a dragon—or perhaps another animal—hurt and in need of help.

He stopped.

The girl looked at him. "What is it?"

"Did you hear it?"

She shook her head. Jasper wondered if he was imagining things or if it was an impression, when he heard it again.

This time she looked scared as if she'd heard it too. "Are we in danger?"

"No, I mean, maybe." She trembled. He added, "I mean, no. You'll be safe." He looked at the direction the scream had come from. His first instinct was to go there and do something, but he was alone, with no equipment or food for the dragons, no first aid kit, and he could be endangering the girl.

"What is it?" she asked.

Jasper sighed. "There's a hurt dragon there."

"And you want to help it."

He thought for a moment. "After you're safe out of this valley. Let's go."

"You can't go in alone, though. It could be dangerous."

"I know." He hated to admit it, but it was true. "I'll come back later, better prepared. Let's get out of here."

As he walked towards the fence and the tower, he still heard a couple of those horrible screams. They sounded muffled and far away. The odd thing was that, other than those screams of pain, he heard no normal sound. Perhaps there was only one creature close enough to them and the others were far away. Perhaps it had been left behind. Had it, though? He had never read that dragons behaved that way, but then, written accounts were often imprecise. There could be so many things happening, but he muffled his curiosity and focused on saving the girl he'd come to save. She was also scared and also needed help. He wished he could do more and wished she could trust him.

They walked for a few more minutes and didn't come across any creatures. There was definitely something wrong in that valley, and he'd come back later to check. When they reached the fence, he used his de-electrifier to stop the current long enough for them to climb out. He didn't fail to notice that the girl was quite fast. Too fast for a farm worker. In fact, her skin was tan, but not as tan as a lot of people on the planet, and he assumed she didn't go out much in the sun. Definitely not a farm worker. He wondered what she did, but kept the question to himself.

When they were away from the fence, he asked, "Can you go back home from here?"

"It's a long walk, but I'll manage it." She smiled. "I've managed much worse." She stared at him with her stunning eyes. "Thanks. And bye."

She was turning when he said, "Wait." The girl stopped and looked at him. "I want to see you again." The words had come out of his mouth of their own accord. He hadn't exactly planned to say that.

Her lips curved up as if to smile, she had a glimmer in her eye, and then she looked down. "I don't know if I should tell you my name—"

"You don't have to. I'll meet you at the market. Near the booth where I first saw you. Tomorrow night. Are you free tomorrow?"

She was startled, but a happy kind of startled. "Yes. Yes, I'm free. You don't mind not knowing my name?"

"Mysterious Girl works. Unless you want to tell me."

She looked down and shook her head.

He said, "Until tomorrow, then."

"See you."

She stared at him again, before turning around and walking through the fields. He followed her with his eyes. She was petite but quite stunning, and there was also something... He wasn't quite sure. The only thing he knew was that he wanted to see her again. He walked back to the tower where Leah had been waiting for him, not looking forward to whatever she was going to say about how long he'd taken or how worried she'd been.

ALANA'S HEART was jumping in her chest as she walked home. She looked back a few times just to make sure that she wasn't being followed, but she wasn't. The first thing was that she was alive. After having almost given up, after everything that had happened to her in space, it was like a miracle to be alive, walking home as if nothing had happened. The second thing was the golden sphere. She'd given it some thought and was sure it would be her chance to change her life for the better. Third, and that hadn't been expected; Jasper. He was so good looking she had trouble breathing around him, let alone talking. Despite her fear of telling him her identity, despite her lack of conversation skills, he wanted to see her again. Would that be a date? It didn't matter. What mattered was seeing him. And then maybe by then she'd have solved her life and would be able to look at him like an equal. Maybe she could hope.

Janet had been shut down for a while, sleeping, or something. At first it annoyed Alana but in the end it had been good. Alana was safe, as Jasper had walked her out of the valley. She wondered if maybe she'd be safe regardless, and if there was something wrong with the dragons, or if they were dying. She'd enjoyed walking with Jasper, though, and maybe it was good that she had some privacy.

When she got home, she hugged her mother like she hadn't hugged in many years.

Her mother smiled but asked, "What's wrong, darling?"

"Wrong? Why is it wrong that I'm hugging you?"

"It's almost as if you feared never seeing me again. You need to stop taking these assignments. You know that."

Her mother was pretty close to the truth, but not quite. Alana smiled. "I am going to stop, I am! Something happened, mama, something happened and we'll be free and we'll go away from this planet."

Her mother sighed. "I like it here."

"You do? We can rarely even buy vegetables."

"Samitri is what I know, darling. But you can go."

"We'll see."

Her mother always said that but she would change her mind once Alana got her the surgery to walk again, once they were in Ringon, in a nice house, with their lives ahead of them.

Alana went to the bedroom and closed the door.

"Janet?"

"I'm here," the little woman replied from the small sphere in her ear.

"I thought you'd been gone or something."

"No. But I only show up when I'm called."

"Oh, I see. I know what I want for my first wish."

"What is it?"

"Six million universal credits." Alana had given it a lot of thought. All that she wanted was freedom and the ability to go away from Samitri. She wanted to change her life. Enough money would allow her to do just that. If she'd asked to go away, or if she'd asked for her mother's operation, she'd spend two wishes instead of one.

"Are you sure that's what you really want? From the bottom of your heart?" Janet asked.

"Pretty sure."

"We start it now, then, and you'll need to do as I say."

"Does it involve jumping into space?"

Janet laughed. "No. Unless you want to. You got a taste for that, right?"

"Looking back, it feels amazing. When I did it, I was terrified."

"You did better than I expected and kept your cool despite your slim chances of survival. I had my doubts for moments."

"Really? But I thought I'd be saved if I did as you told me."

"*If* you did as I told you. You do realize you could have panicked and done something else, right?"

"I'm glad I didn't. And now let's go for the six million!"

To be fair, Alana still had a little doubt in her mind. While escaping the black ship seemed almost impossible at the time, it involved knowledge that Janet had. She couldn't quite imagine how the little woman would find her such a fortune, but she was willing to give it a try.

"When do you want it?" Janet asked.

"As soon as possible."

"Don't you want to rest?"

Indeed. Alana was exhausted. She'd walked for two hours to get home, but that was the least of it. All the tension in space was getting to her muscles.

"Yes, I need to sleep."

"Tomorrow morning, then."

Alana washed then lay down smiling, thinking about finally finding her freedom. Part of her smile was for Jasper too. She didn't want to be a silly girl, and didn't want to get over excited for something that could turn out to be nothing, but at least there was a gorgeous guy who wanted to see her. Why not smile?

———

ALANA WAS TROUBLED by dreams she couldn't quite remember. She'd seen herself back in the Ghost Ship and then in other ships or constructs with similar architecture and spongy walls that swallowed her. She woke up with a start.

"Janet?" she called.

"Yes?"

"Will I get in trouble for having you? I mean, is there a curse or something? Won't someone be angry?"

"You could get in trouble with anything, Alana. But there's no curse, no."

"I dreamed about a ship like the one where I found you."

"It was a shocking experience. You'll probably dream about it for a while."

Alana sat up. "That makes sense."

"Are you ready?"

"For what?"

"Is that a question? Last night you told me your first wish. Let's go get it."

Go get it. Right. She had the guidance but still had to do her part. "Let's go."

"You'd better leave soon, then. There's a cargo ship going to Vereno, and that's where you'll find your fortune."

"I'll have to leave Samitri again?"

"It's the fastest way. This planet doesn't have fortunes lying around."

"And Vereno does?"

"You'll see."

"You can't tell me?" Alana asked.

"No. Trust is part of the process."

"All right."

Alana got dressed, but then she remembered Jasper. "When do you think I'll be back?"

"Couple days at most."

Alana looked down. "I was going to meet someone tonight."

"I hadn't accounted for that. Well, we could wait until next week."

Alana didn't want to wait that much, though, and Jasper was actually one more reason why she shouldn't wait. She didn't know how long he'd stay in this planet, but didn't want to meet him in a position of inferiority. If she got her fortune, things would be much different.

"No. Let's go now. I'll just pass by the market and leave a note for him."

Although rare, her mother had some paper. Alana took one, thought for a while, then wrote a note. She hesitated. Was it too bold? But then, it was so much easier to write than say things, with the disadvantage that the written word would remain as proof. Oh, well, it wasn't as if she was writing that she was in love with him. She passed by the market, left it with Bert, then made it to the docks. Her heart was pounding. She wore sunglasses and had her hair hidden in a hoodie, but she wasn't supposed to be out and about during the day and could be in trouble if someone found her. Things would change soon, though, because

with enough money she would be able to buy a fake identity—and her freedom.

Janet led her to the docks and told her to hide in a laski
transporter. It was a bit disgusting because she was going to
travel with the animals, but it was true that nobody would
be able to find her except with a visual inspection, and she
doubted anyone would come looking for an intruder. The
creatures were in cages and Alana hid behind one of them.
She lay down over her jacket and ended up napping. Two
male voices awoke her. Employees had come to feed the
laskis. Alana paid attention where they moved and tried to
keep far from their view.

Soon they landed. Alana waited and slipped outside
after the back door was opened. This was a cargo port, with
ships being loaded with minerals and semi-precious
stones. Vereno's main activity was mining. With that bleak
dock, Alana tried to imagine who would be rich enough to
afford fresh laski meat, but then, there were probably some
mine administrators. The real owners were probably far
away in Ringon or somewhere else.

Alana still wondered how she was going to make a
fortune there, but she decided to trust Janet and embarked
on an empty cargo train. She watched the sunset from the
small slits in her compartment. This star was more reddish
than Samitri's, and the light gave the planet an eerie,
unnatural tone. Now that it was becoming night, everything was even redder, illuminating cut-off hills and cut-
down forests who had been brought down to make room
for mining.

The trip was long and again she slumbered into weird dreams with dark ships and an alien city, with buildings made of the same dark material as in the black ship.

———

JASPER HAD a lot more trouble than he'd expected to go to the market alone. He had to convince Leah to leave him and had to convince the guards assigned to protect him to stay at a distance. He had the feeling that his mother had a hand on this and that he was being watched. He hadn't had a chance to go to the dragon valley either. That said, just a walk in the market was innocent enough, and, with guards far away, he'd be able to at least talk a little bit with the mysterious girl. He hoped she'd tell him her name because mentally calling her mysterious girl was getting weird. It also meant she didn't really trust him, which was very unfair.

He didn't see her near the point where they had arranged. Perhaps she'd be late. Perhaps she was around here somewhere, disguised because of her intense fear of being recognized. Far away, on a booth, a seller beckoned in his direction. And then again. Jasper decided to check if the man wanted to talk to him.

"Was it me you were calling?"

"Yes, yes," the man said. "You are with the Ringon delegation, right?"

"Yes."

"Here." The man put a paper in Jasper's hands. "Alana sent this to you. She can't come tonight."

"Alana." So that was her name. He took the paper. "Thanks." He then looked at the small dragon figures and their bright colors and long tails. "Are these meant to be realistic?"

"A little. I mean, I can't ask a dragon to sit and model for me."

That made sense. The dragons' skins shouldn't be bright pink and blue, for example, but then, Jasper wasn't sure. The figures were beautiful, though. "You make them yourself?"

"Yes."

Jasper examined the dragons. One of them had semi-precious stones for eyes and was probably the most expensive mini dragon there. "Can I have that one?"

The man was surprised. "This one? Right. I'll wrap it for you. It's three hundred credits."

The man rolled some protective paper around the dragon. He was underselling his work by hundreds of credits. Jasper passed him his card. "Take seven hundred. It's still cheaper than it's worth."

The man hesitated, then passed the card for seven hundred. Jasper could have given him two or three thousand, but he didn't want to humiliate him. He then asked, "How do you know Alana?"

The man stared at him, eyes suspicious. "I'm sure she'll tell you. Here. This is your dragon." He passed him the figure.

Jasper walked away and returned to the palace. Only in his bedroom, he opened the note. He could have opened it earlier but then he'd need to shake the guards and he didn't want to bother.

It said:

JASPER,

I wish I could have come in this paper, and be taken by your hand. My heart is warmed by your kindness. I'll be back in a couple days. Don't go away without saying goodbye. I've never met anyone like you.

JASPER STARED AT THE NOTE. This wasn't exactly a love letter or even a love poem, but it wasn't a note to a friend either. Now at least he knew how to reach her, through the dragon seller, and was more than ever looking forward to meeting her—Alana.

———

AFTER WHAT WOULD COUNT as three days in Samitri, Alana returned. She no longer had to hide. Instead, she boarded a passenger shuttle from Kriasis with her fake identification and a universal bank account. Janet had led her to a buried treasure in an abandoned mine. From there, the work was exchanging piece by piece just enough to get out of Vereno and go to the next planet with big cities and a big enough underground economy to allow her to exchange some more. So far, she had two million in the bank and a few more precious stones in her bag. She'd trade them once she and her mother were out of Samitri. Before that, she hoped to see Jasper—if he still wanted to see her, and if he hadn't left the planet yet.

Alana passed by the market and bought some fruit for her mother. They hadn't eaten any in years. She then went to Bert's booth, her heart pounding.

"Did you give him my note?"

"Yes, I did. He came a few times and asked about you. Yesterday he left this."

It was a metal token. In it, it said; *Grand Ball - Samitri Palace - 12th day, 9th month, 8 o' clock.*

"Is this an invitation?"

Bert nodded. "Yes. And tomorrow is the 12th. I guess someone is going to the palace. A couple of days more and you'd missed it."

Alana felt her cheeks getting hot. "Was it..."

"The blond boy; Jasper. He's a nice fellow, passionate about dragons. Now, what are you doing here? Go home. Your mother is dying with worry."

Alana did so. She wanted to run, to jump, so happy she was. Not only she had enough money to buy her freedom, she was going to a ball. Not only a ball, a ball where Jasper would be. And she would be able to afford a dress.

She opened her door and put the fruit on the table. "Mom, mom! You won't believe it! I have enough money for us to leave Samitri, for your operation, for everything!"

Her mother stared at her. "Darling, I'm so happy for you! But I told you I'm happy here. You can go, I won't mind."

She took her mother's hands. "Mom, no. Imagine both of us in Ringon! We can go to the theatre, you can meet people, read your work. Imagine that. We'll be so happy! And you'll walk again!"

"I'll think about it, but you need to think about it too. Make a new life for you, forget all this. Leave it all behind. I'm too old for a new life, honey."

"You're not old!"

"My life's here."

Alana sighed. She could tell her mother how horrible their life had been, having to share a tiny bedroom and a tiny kitchen, without fresh vegetables or fruit, without freedom, but she didn't want to argue. It was true that, with money, Alana could provide her mother a good standard of living—even in Samitri—if her mother really insisted on staying in this hell hole.

"Think, then. I'll also think." She kissed her mother's cheek and went to the bedroom.

She still hadn't told her mother about Janet, and it wasn't that she was ashamed or thought that her mother would be against it, it was just that, for some reason, she felt it was safer to keep it secret. It would also be safe to get away from this planet as soon as possible, in case that Mara woman learned that Alana had survived the Ghost Ship.

———

ALANA ENTERED the clothing shop for the first time. She didn't hide her face, eyes, or hair on the way. With her fake identity, she would be left alone as if she were a tourist from Vareno. Nobody in the shop had ever seen her either. Maybe it was the same planet, but it was a different world. Of course, had she really wanted to impress at the ball, she'd need to get the dress elsewhere, but it didn't matter, she would do her best. She carried the golden sphere in a bag and had the small sphere in her ear.

The shop owner had only children's clothes her size, but Alana picked the one she thought looked the best. As she went to the dressing room, she said, "Janet, are you there?"

"Yes."

"Can you help me choose?"

"Is it a wish?"

"Are you kidding me? No. As a friend."

"Human fashion is alien to me."

True. Alana looked at herself in a golden dress. She wondered if it was too much. "Just tell me what you think of this dress."

"You look pretty. It does bring out your skin color."

"You think so?"

"I do. But like I said, I have no clue how you guys dress."

"Neither do I."

"Why don't you ask the saleswoman?"

"What am I going to say? That I have no clue how people dress?"

"You are pretending to be a tourist, aren't you? Use that to your advantage."

That was true. She was about to approach the woman when she noticed someone coming in the shop. The dark hair was like Mara's, and Alana entered again the dressing room, her heart pounding.

"I think Mara is here," she whispered. "Can you see if she is?"

"Not really," Janet answered. "Do you want me to check?"

That would probably be another wish. "No, it's fine. I may be imagining things."

Alana peeked outside and saw only the middle-aged saleswoman. She walked out carefully and didn't see anyone else, so she approached the saleswoman. "Do you think this is something people in this planet would wear for a ball?"

The woman frowned. "Well, of course. I wouldn't have given you something inappropriate!"

The woman's anger surprised Alana. "Sorry, it's just that I'm not from here. I'll take it."

The woman raised an eyebrow. "It's three thousand credits; universal."

Right. Because she obviously assumed Alana couldn't pay. Oh, the satisfaction in passing her the chip and taking the dress. Golden it was.

———

More and more Jasper had the feeling that he was being kept prisoner. Leah never again was allowed to take him to the dragon valley, and no transports were available to him. He considered one day just walking there, but he had two new security guards on his tail non-stop. It was almost as if they wanted to prevent him from going there.

He had never heard anything from Alana. He'd left an invitation for the ball but his hopes weren't too high. Oh, well. What difference. He was going to leave soon. The ball was his last hope. It was when Leah would escape with her boyfriend. Jasper would also try to take the opportunity to get to the dragon valley. After that, he'd be off planet. He'd come as a favor to his mother, and he'd done more than enough.

He had chosen a white suit. White in white, like his hair, his skin. Maybe not the best choice to sneak out, but he had a cloak and a hood.

6

THE BALL

Alana's heart pounded as she walked into the palace. Yes, it was different from everything she'd seen before, it was odd to wear a formal dress, and she feared being with people from the high society, but what was getting to her was seeing Jasper. It was silly, she knew it, but knowing she was being silly didn't help. In the days she traveled to get her fortune, she kept remembering him with his kind eyes, soft hands, white hair. Of course, she had no idea if he even liked her or if he even thought about her the same way. Well, that was a good reason to be nervous, because she'd finally find out whether she had a good reason to think about him or not. And the worst is that she couldn't stop herself from dreaming of dancing with him, as if she were a princess from a story.

Fine, the Alliance had ended the monarchy and royalty,

but she wasn't thinking about real royals, but about princesses from stories, who only wore pretty clothes, dreamed, and were loved just because. Now that freedom lay at her feet, and her future was open, she could start to dream. She could even think about what she really wanted for herself. For so long all she did was survive. Still, regardless of what happened, she wanted to see Jasper. Maybe they'd still see each other in Ringon. She hoped so.

The golden sphere was in her purse, but she couldn't talk to Janet now. By herself, walking among strangers, all those rich people she didn't know, made her feel awkward. She wasn't sure if her dress wasn't too exaggerated and wondered if the looks she received were admiration or some slight ridicule. Funny that she had no idea what the difference was. Well, having spent most of her life hidden, knowing how to go in and out of places without being seen, perhaps it wasn't strange that she didn't know what it was to be seen. Speaking of seen, no sign of Jasper yet. She wondered if he even was going to be there or if maybe he had something else to do.

A band played calm music. Alana watched it, but then the musicians stopped and the singer said, "Attention everyone for tonight's hosts; Leah Sera."

A door opened on the far right and a beautiful dark-haired girl entered in a red dress. Samitri governor was Sam Sera. The girl was probably his daughter. Hopefully not his wife, in any case.

The singer then announced, "Jasper Forin."

The name got Alana's attention. A door on the left

opened. It was Jasper, the Jasper Alana wanted to see. He wore a white suit matching his hair. His hair looked like the white in clouds. But why was he introduced as the host? And together with a girl around his age? Jasper's eyes caught Alana's and twinkled. In that multitude, he'd found her.

The singer continued, "We're gathered together to celebrate their engagement."

Alana had the impression that he looked surprised, but she couldn't be sure, as she looked away as soon as she could so that he wouldn't see the disappointment in her face.

Was she right to be disappointed? He'd never told her he didn't want to see her as friends only, he'd never told her he wanted to have anything special with her. Still, the way he'd just looked at her... Alana also realized that Jasper was not in the Ringon delegation, he *was* the Ringon representative in Samitri. No wonder there was a world of difference between them.

She also remembered how she had heard that rich people sometimes take lovers and felt icky. Well, maybe not, maybe he just wanted them to be friends.

As Alana tried to come to terms with this new information, a sight made her insides curl: Mara. Was it her? Or was she imagining things again? That woman had two arms. Among so many people, it was easy to get confused. That was when she saw the woman looking in her direction, saw more of her face, and was certain that it was

Mara. She'd either had grown her arm back or had an impressive prosthetic.

Alana turned and walked outside to a garden. She would need to escape without being seen and hoped Mara hadn't seen her. Oh, Alana was so stupid. The first thing she should have done was run away with her mother. But then, she had to get the money. She looked at the walls around the garden trying to think how to climb one of them without being noticed, when a voice startled her.

"Alana!"

She turned. Jasper was calling her—using her name. It didn't matter anymore. "Congratulations," she said.

"It's not what you think."

"You don't know what I'm thinking."

He looked around. "Come here." He gestured to an area behind hedges.

"I'm fine where I am."

"Please."

Alana sighed. Hiding was a good idea at that moment. She followed him.

He said, "I had no idea this was going to be an engagement party."

She rolled her eyes. "Yeah, how would you know you were engaged? These are not the type of things people discuss beforehand or anything."

"But no. I didn't know it. And it's not even real. It's not. I invited you, and I thought... I hope you're not upset."

"You need to make some bold assumptions to think your future marital status upsets me."

Jasper shook his head. "I didn't mean to make any assumptions. *I'm* upset." He stared at her. "I liked your note."

Alana wished she could dig a hole and hide. Yes, writing was easier than saying, on the other hand, you couldn't just pretend that someone had misunderstood or misheard what you wrote. He could keep the note forever and never forget her idiocy.

Jasper stared at her. "That's a beautiful dress."

Was she even supposed to reply? Maybe he did want her as a lover. It was odd, though, because he looked like a nice guy. Nice. What did Alana even know about guys? All she wanted to do was escape that palace, escape that ball, run home, get her mother, and get out of that planet.

He looked uncomfortable. "And I shouldn't have said it. I'm sorry."

Whatever his motivations were, Alana had better use them. "It's fine. Would you do something for me?"

"Of course."

"I need to get out of here, but I can't go back to the main hall. Do you think you can show me another exit?"

"Are you being followed again?"

"I think so."

He had helped her twice now, and Alana saw no reason why he wouldn't help her again. For him, it was a simple favor. He entered a small door, and she followed. They walked through some hallways and then he entered a bedroom. Alana's stomach sank and she considered running, but not before confronting him. "What's the meaning of this?"

"Do you really want to leave this palace in that golden dress?"

True. Then again, she was very suspicious of his intentions. He opened a closet and pulled a cloak. "See if you can put this over your dress."

Alana put it on. The problem was the puffy skirt, which made the cloak look completely ridiculous.

Jasper shook his head and pointed to a door. "The bathroom is there. You'll have to take off that dress. I don't think I'll have pants that fit you, but you can tie the cloak well."

Alana locked the door from the inside. She'd never seen a bathroom like that. It even had a bathtub, which she didn't think Samitri had, with all the water scarcity and all. But that didn't matter. She took off the dress, put the cloak, and tied it on her waist. The bottom dragged on the floor. Better than nothing. As she opened the door, Jasper had a pair of scissors and cut the rim.

"Do you need to escape the palace or do you need to escape the planet?" he asked as he finished.

"Just the palace—for now. I need to get my mother."

"I see. Listen, Leah is escaping Samitri tonight. You could go with her. I could even come with you."

"Why is she escaping?"

"It's a long story. That's what I was trying to tell you. She and I don't have anything. She's leaving tonight. I wanted to use tonight to go to the dragon valley again, but I'll help you escape instead."

"Why?"

"Because I can help you."

"And where is Leah going?"

"Ringon."

That was exactly where Alana wanted to go, except that this time she no longer needed someone's help to go there. She could buy her way out and pay for her ticket. She shook her head. "It's fine. Just show me the way out of the palace."

"I'll come with you."

"It's not necessary."

"You are afraid someone's following you, and you want to walk to your house alone?"

"As long as they don't see me, there's no problem."

Jasper stared at her, then cocked his head. "Maybe."

He led her to a side door from where she reached the exterior of the palace. She looked back and didn't see anyone around her. She was safe and doubted Mara had seen her. Still, it had been a huge risk going to that ball. Well, how could she have known the woman would be there? Either way, each day in Samitri was a risk, so she had to convince her mother and get out as soon as possible.

And what had she been thinking about Jasper? Still, she felt confused. Part of her wanted to believe him, believe him even when he said he was sorry and that he and Leah weren't really engaged. On the other hand, she'd heard about men lying and manipulating, and that was the kind of lie that he could be telling just to get whatever he wanted from her. It didn't matter. What she had to focus on right now was to make sure she wasn't being followed—she wasn't—and getting out of the planet before Mara found out she was alive and had the golden sphere.

The sound of a shot broke the silence in the narrow alleys of Samitri residential city, in the workers' district. It had come from the direction of Alana's house. She grabbed the taser gun from her purse, dropped all caution, and ran to her house. Before she entered, she heard a sound on her right, then pointed and activated her taser. A man collapsed, gun in his hand. She entered and found the house in disarray.

Alana wished her eyes were deceiving her, that it was some horrible mistake. In the kitchen, her mother, Bert, and Isabelle lay on the ground motionless. It couldn't be. All her dreams lay motionless on the ground, her hopes, everything she ever held dear. It was worse than her worst nightmare.

She knelt by her mother and took her pulse, hoping her eyes were deceiving her, when she heard a male voice behind her: "Dead. Unfortunately. Now, you have something my boss wants."

Alana turned. He had a gun pointed at her, and it wasn't a taser. She was wondering if she could be faster than him when another man came from the bedroom.

"It must be in her purse," he said.

She was shaking in anger. "You didn't have to kill them! They had nothing to do with it."

"They are in peace now and didn't suffer. You should be happy, girl. Now give us what we came for."

And then they would kill her. No. It wasn't that she cared much for her life now, but that she wanted revenge. She put her hand in her purse, touched the sphere, and whispered, hoping Janet would hear it, "Help me get out of here alive."

"You don't need my help for that," Janet replied in the small sphere in Alana's ear.

The man insisted, "Hurry, girl."

Maybe she should have clarified to Janet that she still wanted to keep the golden sphere. Even so, she didn't really see any scenario where she could take both armed men and escape, not now that she had no surprise element.

It was Alana who was surprised, though, as the man in front of her collapsed. She turned and tased the man on her side. Jasper was at the door, a taser gun in his hand. He looked down, saw the bodies, and his chest moved up and down, a horrified expression on his face. "Your fa-family?"

"My mother." It was even difficult to talk. "And friends."

"I'm so sorry."

Alana stared at him. "How did you?"

"I was worried so I followed you. Now come. I really think you need to escape this planet."

Tears ran down Alana's eyes as she clutched her mother's body one last time. But this was no time to grieve. She got up. "Thanks"

"I'll take you to my ship. It's in the port. Leah should come soon, then we'll all leave."

She followed him. To Alana's surprise, his ship was the old ship from where she'd gotten information the very day she'd first met him. That explained the excess security and the alarm system in an inconspicuous ship.

"Stay here," he said. "I'll be right back."

Alana hid in a small compartment just in case. Her mind was whirling and her heart was crushed. How could those men have found her house? Maybe Mara had seen her at the dress shop or at the ball. Her world had just fallen apart. Alana had gotten her fortune, and still, it was meaningless, lonely, and sad. She'd been so happy just a few hours before, and now...

After a long time, she whispered, "Janet?"

"Yes?" the little woman replied.

Alana's words were tight. "Why didn't you warn me?"

"I didn't know it. I focus on what you want. I can't focus on everything."

"I wanted to leave this planet with my mother."

"Why didn't you ask for that?"

"Because I needed the money."

"Oh, Alana!" Janet's voice was full of pity. "And now, what do you need?"

"Right now I just want to escape."

"I can help you with that."

"Would I be using a wish?'

"Well, yes."

Alana shook her head. "It's fine. I'll save my wishes for my revenge."

"You need to be alive first."

"I'm hiding. Nobody will find me."

"Alana..." Janet said as if in a warning.

"Wait," Alana whispered. "I think I hear someone."

Other people wouldn't hear Janet, but she wanted to check who was coming.

"Alana?" It was Jasper's voice, with a tinge of panic.

She left the compartment where she'd been hiding.

He exhaled and put his hand on his heart. "I thought... How did you fit there?"

Alana shrugged. There was a girl and a young man behind Jasper.

He pointed at them. "This is Leah and Mike. They're coming with us."

Alana stared at the couple. They were holding hands. So what Jasper had told her was true. Amidst all her sadness, this was a small consolation, even if her crushed heart wasn't ready for romantic thoughts. Her eyes met Jasper's, and he walked towards her.

"I'm sorry. For what happened to you. I wish I could do something..."

"You are."

He sighed. "Let's go, then."

"Wait," Leah said. "I forgot something."

"Leah!" Jasper yelled.

The girl opened the door and got out. Jasper ran after her—and stepped back. Leah was entering the ship with someone else behind her. Alana's blood froze. It was Mara with the three men that had attacked her. Alana stared at Jasper, but he had his eyes fixed on the dark-haired woman.

"Mom? What are you—" He noticed the men and stepped in front of Alana. "Don't hurt her."

He was her son? And he knew where her house was. Was it possible to feel even worse about something? But what Alana had to do was find a way out of that situation. Mara and the three men were armed. Alana's taser was in her bag. She'd have no time to do anything.

"Jasper, Jasper," Mara said. "I know you prefer animals to people, but I wasn't aware you kept company with worms. But thanks for finding her for me." She turned to her men. "Kill them."

Jasper stepped back as if to shield Alana. The guards didn't shoot Jasper, though. They shot Mike. Leah screamed and ran in his direction, but before she reached him, she was also shot and they both dropped dead on the floor.

"What did you do that for?" Jasper yelled. "She had already helped you! Why?"

Alana couldn't see Mara, but she heard her voice. "It doesn't look good for my son to be betrayed. It'll look nicer if his beloved dies a tragic death in the hands of a known criminal who murdered her own family. "

Alana shivered.

Mara continued, "Now, get away from her or I'll have to hurt you."

"No way," he replied.

Jasper then collapsed backwards, and Alana held him. He was still breathing, though, and she noticed that a guard had a taser.

"Wait!" Alana yelled. "The sphere won't work if you hurt me." It was a desperate try, but it was all she had.

"What are you saying?" the dark-haired woman asked.

"You want the golden sphere, right?" She wished she could claim she didn't have it, but they'd probably search her purse. "If you hurt the previous owner, it won't obey you. It won't work. You can't hurt me."

Mara laughed. "Nice tale, girl. Now, since you're in a giving mood, where's the sphere?"

If only Alana had a decoy, something. How stupid she'd been. She lay Jasper on the floor, opened her purse, took the sphere and tossed it to the woman.

In the woman's hand, the blue light came up immediately. This was bad. The woman recited words in a language Alana didn't understand, then asked Janet, "Infinite Sphere, tell me, who is your master?"

"You are," Janet replied.

Alana felt a small pang of betrayal, but she knew it was not the little woman's fault. And she still had the smaller sphere in her ear. Maybe it could still be useful.

Mara asked, "Is it true that I must not harm the little vermin standing there?" She pointed to Alana.

"It is true," Janet replied.

Alana held back the relief sigh that had formed in her chest.

Mara had an icy smile. "I'll treat her well, then. Guards, chain her."

This was Alana's opportunity to try to escape. She ran to the door but collapsed before she got there.

———

ALANA WOKE up in a room in a strange spaceship. It seemed to be a large transport ship, based on the room design. Her door was locked. Of course. She was a prisoner.

"Janet?" she whispered.

Silence was her only answer. She sighed. At least she was still alive, which only made her remorse gnaw on her. If only she'd refused Mara's assignment, if only she'd come to Samitri and escaped right away... What would she do with her money now? If she had any money. Mara was probably powerful and would be able to find her fake identity and confiscate her funds. Alana's purse wasn't in the room either. The remaining precious stones were also gone. It turned out that the fortune Alana had always wanted ended up being useless. Useless to grant her freedom, useless to save her mother, useless to do anything. Regret was all she felt.

A screen popped up in her room with Mara's face.

"Darling, darling, did you have a good sleep?"

Alana just stared.

"I'm here as a friend. Yes, I'll keep you alive and unharmed, but know that I'll keep you. Did you think you could fool me?" She laughed. "And Jasper, just so you know, he also helped me. You should never have crossed me."

"Of course. I would have been so much better left behind in the Black Ship."

Mara had a faint smile. "Definitely. You would just die, instead of being locked up forever, and your family would have been still alive. Big, big, big mistake, girl. But I can make your life easier. See? There's a small part that I need, and I know you have it. Give it to me, or tell me where it is, and I might give you something to eat."

"If you starve me to death, the sphere won't work."

Mara shook her head. "No starvation, don't worry. I just won't be giving you anything—you know—tasty. If you don't eat it, it's your fault only."

As if on cue, a compartment opened on the wall. Raw liver. Mara would need to do much better than that if she wanted to convince Alana to give her the small sphere. Interesting that it should make any difference.

Mara continued, "If you don't want to tell me, it's fine. I can find someone in Ringon to grab that information from you. See? Crossing me is never a good idea."

The screen was off. So she was finally going to Ringon. That had been her dream for as many years as she remembered dreaming something. She would never have guessed how much she would hate it. The image of her mother, and not only her mother, Bert and Isabelle, all gone, was stuck in her mind. They had done absolutely nothing and didn't deserve that. All Alana's fault. She lay down again and dozed off.

She was awoken with the door opening. Jasper was there, finger over his mouth.

"I'm going to help you escape," he whispered.

"How?"

"Escape pod."

"I'll be floating in space, or Mara will come back and find me."

He shook his head. "A spaceship will get you. But it needs to be now while you're at the right coordinates."

Alana's thoughts went to the golden sphere. "Jasper, before I go, do you think you could bring me back my... my things?"

"There's no time. I can look for them later. I'll meet you in Ringon." He stopped in front of the door to the escape pod. "I'm sorry for what my mother did."

"Thanks for helping me."

They walked carefully outside, then to the escape pod door. He opened it, and she entered.

"Go," he said.

The door was closed and the pod was in space before she came up with anything to say.

Again she was floating aimlessly in space, this time with metal around her, not only a spacesuit. Jasper really did try to help her. She hoped she would see him again and felt some relief in the thought that she still hoped for something.

She must have spent about an hour floating when a ship approached the pod. It looked like a very old transport ship, not like the Samitri ships which transported meat or even livestock, but smaller. It had an entrance for the kind of pod she was in. The door opened to a grizzled man with a thick scar across his jaw. He checked a number in the pod, then turned to Alana, "Welcome!"

His appearance was rugged and tough, and Alana felt afraid. Sure, she'd seen people like him before, especially at the Blood Tavern, and sometimes in the port, but she'd never been alone in a spaceship with someone like that.

"Don't be afraid, girl," he said. "We wouldn't harm you either way, but we have a strict contract and we'd need to be crazy to break it."

"What contract?"

"From whoever wants us to keep you alive."

Jasper. Alana stepped out of the pod airlock, entered an empty cargo area then followed the man to the bridge. There was another man there. This one was bald, wearing leather pants and a jacket, with tattoos in his neck and hands.

Alana said, "Thanks for rescuing me."

The bald man shrugged. "No need to thank us. That's what we do; transport stuff. You're our stuff now."

"Angel," the grey-haired man said, as if in a warning.

The bald man called Angel replied, "I mean it's our job."

"This is Angel, I'm Flick. We're taking you to Ringon."

Thieves. Alana knew those kinds of names. She made the sign her father had taught her, closing her right hand and punching the palm of her left twice. "I'm the Black Mouse."

The men stared at each other. Angel said, "So you take things for a living? I'm wondering what you found this time that made you worth a fortune."

Flick stared at his companion. "We're not supposed to ask her any questions."

"C'mon!" Angel raised his hands. "We're asking as

friends, colleagues, let's say. And she doesn't have to answer."

Alana was curious about something else. "You have a contract forbidding you to ask me questions?"

Flick nodded. "Among lots of things. Quite insulting, frankly, but then, people are scared."

"You can ask questions, though," Alana said. "Otherwise it's going to be boring. What do you mean I'm worth a fortune?"

"They are paying really well to see you safe in Ringon. Above what a task like this is worth, contract notwithstanding."

Alana was curious. "How much?"

They looked at each other. "Can we disclose it?" Flick asked.

Angel shrugged.

"Four million universal credits."

Alana was stunned. "Just to get me to Ringon? Wow, your job pays well."

Flick laughed. "Get you to Ringon unharmed. It doesn't usually pay as much, no."

"You could retire after this, right?"

"Not really. It's enough to get a better ship, start getting decent jobs. Maybe take a vacation for some months. Life's expensive."

Alana was stunned. She'd been sure that she'd be able to live the rest of her life without working if she had two million credits, and she was sure that she had a fortune with her six million credits—now gone. Something else was strange. "Who's paying that much?"

"If you don't know it, how are we supposed to know?"

Jasper? Well, he or one of his parents was part of the Peace Alliance. Still, that was a lot. "Who are you going to deliver me to?"

"Neutral space. Anonymous," Flick said.

Alana was thankful that she was being taken care of.

Angel put earphones, listened to something, then laughed. "Check it out: the Alliance Police is looking for you. They have a three million prize for whoever brings you in. That explains the high price. What did you do, girl?"

Alana shrugged. "No idea." She didn't want to disclose that much and had another question. "If the prize they were offering was more than four million, would you hand me in?"

"Maybe," Angel said. "We're also risking getting arrested by not handing you over to the police."

Flick shook his head. "We could try to negotiate with our first client. Flaking on contracts is not good business either."

Alana didn't say anything, but she was afraid to the extent Mara would go to find her. Maybe she should have given her the small sphere. But it wasn't right. That woman didn't deserve it. What Alana had to do was get back the big sphere. In a way, it had been her fault for finding it and taking it out of the Ghost Ship.

Her heart was also sinking thinking about her mother.

She didn't even know if anyone would dispose of the bodies properly. Perhaps some neighbors. All of that because of her mistake, when all that she'd wanted had been to give her mother freedom. Instead of being sad, Alana focused on getting her revenge against Mara. For the kids she'd killed, for her mother, for Bert, for Isabelle.

They'd been silent for a while when Flick turned to her. "We have a little problem, girl."

"What is it?"

"We have to land at an interplanetary dock. We have no choice. But they're in lockout."

"What does it mean?"

"The police are examining every ship before anyone can get out. They are probably looking for you. I can't really find our contact. Do you know any way to reach him or her?"

"Why?"

"We were thinking of going back to some planet where there won't be as much police. If not... We'll have to hand you in and get the reward. I'm sorry."

"No. No. I can hide."

He shook his head. "They'll search everywhere."

"Not where it's too small. I can fit in a small compartment. A small box, something." She had to think fast, and hope to convince them, also fast. "Under the pilot seat there's usually a compartment for an emergency parachute, but most ships don't really have one, so there should be a space there—quite small. They won't look for me there."

He looked incredulous. "Under the seat? Well, you can try..."

Angel got up and showed the space beneath his seat. "You think you can fit *here*?"

"Let me see." Alana folded her knees, then curled her back. Angel put the seat back on, and she was enveloped in darkness.

Angel took out the seat, and Alana got out with much difficulty.

The bald man nodded. "That works, but how are you supposed to get out of the ship and port?"

"They'll inspect it once, right? Once they don't find anyone, they'll let you leave with your boxes. I can go in one."

"You're lucky you're so small, girl."

"I know."

Flick was chewing some kind of dried meat. He noticed she was staring, and said, "Do you want some?"

Alana nodded and took a large strip of meat. She'd never had anything like that before. "This is good."

Angel snorted. "Good? This tasteless crap?"

"It's muscle meat. It's expensive."

The men stared at each other.

"What?" Alana asked.

"Where are you from? I mean, if you don't mind asking, and if you won't tell your benefactor we were too intrusive."

At this point, they could probably find all the information they wanted in the police report. "Samitri."

"Oh, I see, you're so used to the juicy, fresh laski meat, that you think this is some kind of delicacy."

"We don't eat the meat, though. Just the guts. I had meat I think only once or twice when I was a kid." The men had an odd look. "What? It's normal, right?"

"You're from the meat-producing planet and never had meat?"

"Not muscle meat. We ate the guts." The men still had a face. "It's really good."

Angel shrugged. "If you say so. Meanwhile, you can have as much as you want from our dried meat. At least while it lasts."

THEY LANDED in Ringon a couple hours later. Alana didn't see anything, since she'd hidden in the compartment when they were well beyond the planet's atmosphere, seeing from a distance the magnificent rings that gave the planet its name.

One thing she hadn't considered was that there wasn't much air circulation in that little space. Sure, it wasn't sealed, so some air could come in and out, but it wasn't open either, and she was feeling like she was going to suffocate, not to mention the discomfort in her body. Perhaps she'd never been in such a tight spot, but then, her life had never depended on it so much.

Minutes and minutes passed until she heard footsteps and voices of a boarding party examining the ship. She even heard some barking. Hopefully the dogs didn't know her smell and were only looking for someone alive. Angel sitting on top of her would be enough human smell for the dog owners not to know there was anyone under the seat. She trusted that the search party would not expect anyone to be hiding there, and people base their actions, deductions, and conclusions on their assumptions. Even if a dog sniffed in her direction, the person's logic would tell them that they were just sniffing Angel. Or so she hoped.

More time passed, the voices quieted down, then she finally saw the seat removed from above her and took a deep breath with fresh air. This was really fresh, not just the stale artificial ship air.

Angel and Flick looked at her. "Sorry but you're going in another box."

"I hope it's bigger this time."

Angel shook his head. "Too risky. You'll be safer if nobody thinks a person could be in there."

That was true, but the ship had already been searched. "Is the security that tight?"

"It is."

Mara really wanted Alana and was a lot more powerful than she'd expected.

Flick pushed a cart with wheels and a few metal boxes over it. Alana got into one just tight enough for her, then heard other boxes being put above and around her.

At least those guys were good at their job. A lot of people would have quit when they heard about police involvement. Getting the reward the Peace Alliance was paying would have been a lot easier and less risky. On the other hand, delivering her like they'd first agreed paid more—and they would keep their reputation and finish their assignment.

Alana was pushed and carried around. It was odd that she was finally in Ringon and couldn't see anything of its capital. She tried not to think about her mother because regret didn't help. She was in a vehicle now, wondering how long she'd need to be folded like that.

"Alana?" Janet's voice came in her ear.

"Janet!"

"Listen, I can't talk for long. I managed to convince my master that she needs the smaller sphere, and I managed not to tell her where it is, but I won't be able to keep convincing her for long."

"But that's why she's after me."

"I had no choice. You don't understand. Mara must not use me, she must not." Her voice trembled and cracked. "What she wants to do is beyond the worst that I could ever imagine. She would ruin humanity and the blues."

"The blues still exist?"

"Of course we do. Now listen, please, you have to get me back and get me away from my master."

"How can I do it?"

"Mara's going back to Samitri. You'll want to go there."

"I just escaped there. You want me to go straight back into danger?"

"You're the only one I can talk to, Alana. You escaped Mara. That was what mattered. You could get help. Ah, and it has something to do with the dragons. You'll be able to convince Mara's son. It's important. I have to go."

The idea of returning to Samitri wasn't pleasant and she wasn't sure she'd be able to convince Jasper or get anyone to help her. That sphere had to be taken out of that woman's clutches, though. Hearing Janet and knowing that she'd have some of her guidance encouraged Alana to at least try something. Once she was free, of course. Right now she was in a tight box, unable to do anything for anyone.

After a long time, the top of the box was opened, and Alana saw Angel's face.

"You can get out."

This time she almost thought she would get stuck, as she had difficulty unbending her back and knees. Angel and Flick pulled her hand.

"This is it," Flick said.

Alana looked around. She was in a completely white room with two couches and one door. "What is this?"

"A delivery station. Fancy stuff. Your benefactor or someone sent by him or her should come and pick you up. Before that, they'll ask you some questions."

"You mean I can't get out?"

The men looked at each other, and Flick said, "No. It's a delivery, right? We only get paid once you're delivered, and this is a neutral place to make sure we all comply with the terms."

Interesting.

"But you should be fine," Flick said.

Angel said, "Something else, girl. You should change your name."

"For what?"

"Jack-in-the-box."

Alana laughed. "Mice also fit in tight spaces, though. But I'll consider it."

"It was nice transporting you." Flick said.

"Thanks." She felt scared, afraid of being left alone in that place. "Wait, is there any way I can contact you? Or you could contact me? I mean, you see, I can do things nobody else can. If you ever need someone, or if you know someone who could use someone like me..."

"We'd be delighted to help," Flick said. "But you're worth millions. We don't know many people who deal with those values."

"But that's just now. I'm not the one paying millions for me, and I don't know about tomorrow. I'll need to find work."

Angel nodded. "You know our code names, and we know yours. You'll be able to find us where people look for, let's say, unusual transport."

She'd need to figure it out, but perhaps her experience with signs and underground work in Samitri could help her. "Thanks."

"Goodbye."

The men turned around and left. Never before she'd felt so lonely. She thought that maybe Jasper would come to see her, but he'd probably free her and then go live his life. She had a glimmer of hope that maybe she could find work here. Surely there would be lots of ships and even buildings where someone as small as her could make a difference. Maybe she could start over. From zero. She'd always complained so much about her life, and yet, she had a house, a family, a bed. Now she had nothing. She also had to figure out how to go back to Samitri and get Janet back. The issue was how to do that from nothing.

A huge screen flickered on the wall. Alana trembled as she remembered Mara, but what she saw was an artificial face. A mechanical voice said, "Please sit on the armchair and stare straight forward. I will ask some questions. Please answer as best as you can, and try not to lie."

Alana sat. "I'm ready."

"Were you physically harmed in your journey with your intermediates?"

"Intermediates?"

"The men who brought you."

"Oh. No. Why—"

"It's procedure," the artificial face said on the screen. "Did they ever made you uncomfortable?"

Alana's back was killing her, but it wasn't Angel and Flick's fault. "No."

"Why the hesitation? And potential lie?"

Alana sighed. "Not lie. I had to hide and be in an uncomfortable position, but it was necessary. My, uh, intermediates, didn't have a choice. It was to save my life."

"I see. I'll rephrase. Did they ever made you psychologically uncomfortable?"

"No."

"Did they touch you?"

"Robot face, you're getting creepy. We might have shaken hands, but I'm not sure."

The artificial face took a moment, as if computing. "Did they ask any intrusive questions?"

"No!" Alana yelled. She was annoyed at the lack of trust and horrible assumptions made against the two men who had been nice to her. "They were fine, they brought me here, they were nice."

The screen went back to blank. A few seconds later, the door opened. Jasper came in. He rushed to her and hugged her. "You're fine. I can't believe it. I was so afraid. With the police and everything, I feared they wouldn't get you here."

It was strange to be hugged like that. Until then, they had been just acquaintances. It felt good, though. More than ever, she needed someone to hold her. She leaned in and hugged him back. Her face reached his chest and she could hear his heart. She was about to break down and cry when she remembered what Janet had said about her need to go to Samitri, Mara, the dragons. Alana had to hold it together.

"Jasper, I need to talk to you. In private."

He nodded. "Come."

He walked out the door and it led to a corridor with two doors. He entered one of them. It was a black room.

"This is isolated," he said.

"Are you sure?"

"Pretty much. This is the most prestigious delivery facility in Ringon."

Alana didn't trust it that much. "But information is worth a lot." Alana would know, having worked on retrieving classified information for so long.

"And so is providing a safe place for information exchange."

"All right." Would there be any place where she would be certain not to be heard? Alana looked at him. "There's a lot I need to tell you."

She told him everything. The work she used to do in her planet, her meeting with Mara, her experience in the Black Ship, how she escaped, the sphere, and why Mara was chasing her. It was awkward to tell those things to her son, but Alana felt she could trust him. She then told him what Janet had just told her.

Jasper had been staring in silence, a shadow in his eyes, especially when she mentioned the dead children in the Ghost Ship. He said, "And you think you can trust this Janet?"

"I think I can."

"True, but according to what you're saying, now she works for my mother. She could be doing it to lure you there. It could be a trap, Alana."

"What about the dragons? Did you ever find out what was wrong with the valley?"

"No. It was as if they wanted to keep me out."

"So there could be something there. Jasper, please. I know she's your mother, but we saw some of what she's capable of. If she keeps that sphere... We have to get it back."

Jasper took a deep breath. "First let's confirm if my mother is really there. She didn't say anything about leaving Ringon, but I'll check that. Second, I'll call some friends to come with us. For the dragons."

"That means we're going?"

"That's what you want, isn't it?"

Somehow she felt embarrassed that he would be doing something just because she'd asked. "Yes."

"Then we go." Jasper bit his lip. "I need to find a way to get you out of here, though. There are pictures of you everywhere."

"I came in a box. I can go out in it. Nobody will suspect there's a person in it."

Jasper frowned, as if suspicious.

Alana insisted, "That's how I got here."

"If I had known, I would have chosen a remote planet. I thought... I thought you'd be free once you were out of the ship. I never thought my mother would be so insistent on getting you."

"It's the sphere." Something clicked on her. "Why are you helping me?"

He flushed. His skin was so light that it became easily pink. "It's my mother's fault. I feel responsible." He then seemed to want to change the subject. "Show me that box." They walked to the other room and he looked around. "It must be gone. There's only this small—"

Alana walked to the box and knelt in it.

Jasper stared at her, eyes wide. "You're kidding, right?"

"That's how I wasn't found. Now I'd rather hurry out of here to some place where nobody will find me."

"Maybe Samitri will be the last place she'll look."

Just then Alana realized something. "There's something odd, though. How did she know I was coming to Ringon?"

"Maybe she didn't. Maybe there's security in every planet."

"There isn't, though, and they wanted to bring me to another planet. The only reason they didn't was that they couldn't contact you."

Jasper closed his eyes. "She might have guessed I'd meet you."

"You were probably followed, then. Once we're out of here, I'll be caught."

"Even if all I'm doing is carrying a box?"

Alana shrugged. "They would be curious, wouldn't they?"

"Get out of the box. There's something we can do before we leave. I'll be right back."

Alana sat on the couch, her stomach in a knot. Of course Mara suspected that her son would help her. That was what he'd been doing last time she'd seen them. She probably knew Jasper had released her.

Jasper came in and asked for Alana to follow him.

They came to a place with mirrors, droids, and instruments that looked like combs and scissors. There were also seats with basins on the back.

"We'll have to change our hair color. The length also. It will help. I'm very visible with my hair, but you're not much better. That's a huge heap of hair for someone as tiny as you."

Alana touched her hair, surprised and hurt that he should talk about it like that.

Jasper approached her and touched her hair. "It's gorgeous. That's what I mean. It's beautiful hair, quite memorable. But right now, that's a problem."

Alana nodded, now feeling her cheeks getting hot. Her own consolation was that she wasn't fair enough to blush.

Jasper touched his own hair. "What color do you want?"

It was sad that he would no longer look like he had clouds on his head. "It's up to you."

"We'll have to look different, remember that."

Alana sat on her chair. The droid showed her some samples of colors and styles. She'd never been in a salon before, either regular or droid-operated. Her mother was the one who trimmed her ends. The thought stung. She'd give everything to have her mother back again cutting her hair.

THE GIRL STARING at her in the mirror was almost a stranger. She had straight, light brown hair to the chin. A few minutes later, a brown-haired boy walked in. Jasper. His hair had been cropped short, and he'd dyed not only his hair but his eyebrows and eyelashes as well.

"You look different," she said.

"Do you like it?"

"I preferred it before." She then added quickly, "Not that it's bad now."

"It's funny. My mother always wanted me to dye my hair. In her words, she wanted me to hide my *condition*. I never let her. Well, at least since I got old enough to make my own choices." He looked at Alana. "I also preferred you before, but you're still beautiful. I'm sorry, it will grow back."

"As long as I'm alive."

"True. Now get in that box. How long can you spend there?"

She'd spent about an hour in it, and her entire body hurt. At the same time, it was better to feel pain than to be dead or worse. "One hour, two hours. I could spend more if necessary."

"I'll try to be quick. You said the men who brought you were competent?"

"Yes, they were nice and professional."

Alana entered the box. Before closing it, Jasper asked, "Are you sure it doesn't hurt?"

What a question. Of course being squeezed and bending her body like that hurt. She didn't want to worry him, though, and at that moment, safety was more important than comfort. "I'm fine."

ALANA WAS out of the box in what seemed like an eternity afterwards. She found herself back in Flick and Angel's ship, with Jasper reaching out his hand to her.

"We're going to Samitri?"

"Not directly, but yes. Come. There's a kitchen here. We need to eat something."

Alana followed him. It was weird to see him without his white-blond hair, but on the other hand, now she paid more attention to his face. He'd look good with any type of hair. Alana had to be careful not to confuse his kindness with something more, though. And yet, that night at the ball he'd been so insistent on apologizing, saying he had nothing with Leah... And that hug, she could almost still feel it. Still, he was an heir of the Peace Alliance. Alana was—nothing right now. She'd been a thief, but wasn't even sure if she could be hired again in Samitri or if she'd ever find a job anywhere else. There was a huge divide between them and she had to keep that in mind before getting carried away with feelings that would only cause her pain.

"What are you thinking?" he asked as they sat down.

"A lot. So much has happened."

He looked down then back at her. "I know. I'll do all I can to make it up for you. I mean, I know it won't, but—"

"I appreciate it."

It sounded cold, distant, wrong, but she wasn't sure what else to say. Jasper smiled and held her hand. Alana gasped in surprise. Jasper removed his hand, looked away, got up, then walked to the door.

"Wait!" Alana pleaded. "I'm sorry."

He turned. "For what?"

She wanted to say she was sorry for making him move

his hand away from her, but she wasn't sure how to word it. "Stay. I like your company."

She swallowed, afraid maybe she'd said too much.

Jasper smiled. "I'm just going to see where we are. I'll be right back."

———

THEY STOPPED IN SILOS, a tiny planet, mostly a commercial hub. Alana and Flick stayed in the ship while Jasper and Angel went out to get some supplies. Alana still felt that horrible hollowness, regret, but she focused on the task ahead, on the idea of getting back the golden sphere, defeating Mara. There was the awkward problem that she was Jasper's mother, though, but it wasn't as if Alana wanted to kill the woman.

Flick sat beside her, "So *that* was your benefactor."

"Yes."

He laughed.

Alana asked, "What's funny?"

Flick shook his head. "Me and Angel, we were trying to unscramble our heads to understand why you were so valuable. The answer is obvious."

"Is it?"

"Don't tell me you don't know it, girl, because doubting and not knowing have caused people too much unnecessary heartache."

He must have thought Jasper was romantically interested in her. Her first instinct was to deny it, but then she'd need to tell a very complicated story of a son trying to make up for his murderous mother. Alana attempted a smile. "I'll keep that in mind."

They came back with new clothes and some other supplies. Alana was glad to change out of that cloak and put on pants and a shirt. They were big for her, but she rolled the rims. Jasper eyed her up and down as she came out of the room. "Is it good?"

"Better than a cloak."

He nodded. "Angel suggested I get you child's clothes and pretend you're my little sister."

That sounded like a smart idea, except that something about it felt weird, awkward, and wrong. Still, it was smart. "Why didn't you?"

He stared at her. "It would be quite disturbing. And I don't think it's necessary. I got fake IDs, and we'll meet my friends at the dragon valley. Nobody should look at us twice."

That was probably true. There were the rare but occasional tourists in Samitri, plus all the transport ships. It was unlikely that they would spare two strangers any look. His new hair helped a lot.

There was only one problem. "What about security in the port?"

"We aren't landing there."

7

DRAGONS

Jasper watched Alana jump the ship as it hovered over the dragon valley, then he jumped after her. The planet was already turning away from its sun, so they'd need to look for whatever they had to look at night. She'd wanted him to come to this valley, and it had been his wish as well, so it made sense to be here. This time he was prepared with calming gas bombs, tranquilizing darts, and two tasers.

He walked to the tower where he should meet his friends, Alana beside him. He wondered if he should take her hand, but feared it wasn't what she wanted. Perhaps he'd come here just so as to stretch his time with her for as long as possible. He feared that she'd just walk away and disappear in Ringon, or that she'd hate him because of his mother. She didn't hate him, but he didn't know how much she liked him either.

There was something else bothering him. As much as he'd never gotten along with his mother, he'd never have guessed that she could murder somebody in cold blood or leave a girl on a ship to die. He wasn't sure if he believed that the dead children Alana had seen in the alien ship had been sent by his mother. Still... it opened a hole in his chest and gnawed at his insides. Part of him even envied Alana, who had lost her mother but who could continue to love her, but it would be horribly selfish to say any of that. All he could do was make up for his mother. Part of Alana's grief was his own grief.

It also felt good to be near Alana. Tiny as she was, she was fierce but also had fear and vulnerability, reminding him of the tigers in Firis. He'd obviously never mention it to her. He also knew that she wasn't a wild defenseless cub, and that it would be her choice whether he'd ever be able to care for her. So far she'd been allowing him, though. He could almost believe she liked it, which was a small consolation in his world that had been shattered.

They approached the tower where his friends were going to show up. A voice said, "Who's there?"

"It's me; Jasper." He approached them, and to his disappointment saw only two people; Gala and Martel.

Martel said, "I didn't recognize you." He pointed to Jasper's head. "The hair."

"That's good. Where are the others?"

Martel shook his head. "Couldn't come."

Jasper introduced Alana to them and them to Alana with that awkwardness at saying "she's my friend" when in fact she wasn't exactly a friend because he hadn't known her for long and he didn't think of her like that.

Gala passed him night vision binoculars and asked, "What are we dealing with here?"

Jasper shook his head. "I don't know."

She pointed to Alana. "Is she trained?"

In rescuing animals, she meant. "No, but I can take care of her."

"Let's investigate," Martel said.

Jasper put his hand on Alana's shoulder. "Are you all right? I could bring you to the city."

"I'd rather not be anywhere—" she hesitated, looking at his companions. "Where I can be found. Plus, you know, there's something I want to find here..."

He nodded and squeezed her shoulder. "You'll be safe with me."

She had a small smile, and he knew it meant a lot with all that she was going through. Her trust also meant a lot.

———

Alana didn't hear Janet anymore, but, as she followed Jasper and his friends, she had the impression that there was something odd going on in the valley.

Gala stopped and looked at the ground. "It looks like tire marks."

Martel took a flashlight, but Jasper gestured for him to stop. "We're safer in the dark." He knelt and nodded. "It looks like it's going in that direction." He pointed towards the middle of the valley.

"We should just light the ground," Martel said. "This is not clear either way."

Jasper put a finger over his mouth. "I hear someone."

He gestured for them to hide behind a rock formation.

Gala whispered, "Don't you mean something?"

"Someone."

Jasper passed a taser gun to Alana. "You know how to use it, right?"

He had a funny smile and probably remembered their first meeting as well as she did. His calm eyes eased her embarrassment. Would a tiny taser like that work on a dragon, though? Then she heard it. The sound was a thud, thud, very clearly a person walking.

Jasper jumped from his hiding spot and in a couple seconds immobilized a man on the ground.

"Easy, Jasper," Gala said.

She was mistaken because the man dropped a projectile gun. That kind could shoot ten projectiles per second. Had Jasper not been fast, the man could have killed them all. Alana picked up the weapon while Gala and Martel stared.

"What are you doing here?" Jasper asked the man.

"Security. Security, boy. It doesn't look good for people to die here."

"Really? If there are dragons out to kill people, how come you're walking alone, without equipment?"

The man laughed. "I never said dragons." He then tried to push Jasper, but was tased before he could do anything.

Alana sighed. "He'll wake up and alert whoever he's working for."

"Not necessarily," said Martel. He had a syringe in his hand. He knelt and applied an injection on the man. "Tranquilizer. He'll have a nice sleep."

"Let's hide him."

They pulled his sleeping body behind the rocks. It wasn't the best hiding spot, but at least it was away from the tracks. He had a communicator and some ID, which Jasper confiscated. Alana tried to think back to everything she learned about sneaking and hiding.

"We need to get away from this path. Try to find someplace where we won't be seen as easily."

"The woods there," Jasper said.

They walked away from the place where they'd seen car tracks, and were now among trees, taking a long cut towards the direction where they thought something was happening. They hadn't seen any dragons or other creatures so far.

After walking for about an hour, they saw a glimmer in the sky, as if there was light coming from the ground in a lower part of the valley. They couldn't really see much from where they were, and Jasper suggested approaching it alone.

Alana shook her head. "No way. If we run into somebody again, and if they are more than one, you could be in trouble alone."

Jasper nodded. They all crawled towards the light. They came to a cliff. Below it, there were a few houses, and pens as far as the eye could see. At first, Alana thought they were really huge Laskis, but then she realized what she was looking at: dragons. Their skins had many colors, like blue, purple, red, and they had large scales and wings. The sight was almost hypnotizing.

But she had to focus. There were security towers around the area with armed men on top of them. Alana was wondering how they even got there, when she saw, far away, that there were some ships stationed.

Martel whispered, "We'll need to get help and come back. Tell the Alliance Police"

Alana shuddered, remembering that this same police had been looking for her and were probably still looking.

Jasper nodded as if agreeing with his friend. Was he crazy? Alana held his arm. "I need to go there."

"What can you even do?"

"Get back something that's mine." She had the impression that the golden sphere—and Mara—were there.

"They're not going to be there. I doubt my, uh, she even knows this place."

Alana whispered to Jasper only, "And you think the Alliance Police doesn't know this place? You think they wouldn't have noticed ships coming in the planet without being in the official records?"

"Maybe. But we can't do anything."

Alana looked down again at that valley. There were tiny houses and buildings, yes, but there was also a bigger building, closer to the ships. If Mara—and Janet—were there, that was where they would be.

"I can sneak in, get what I need, and get out." He didn't look convinced. "Look," Alana insisted, "maybe the Alliance police doesn't know about this place. Fair enough. But if we alert them, and if by any miracle they do come, don't you think these people will have escaped before they can be caught? Mara has influence over them. She'll know."

Jasper was annoyed. "She can't have anything to do with these dragons."

"I'll just check. I'll go in and out. It's my specialty."

"They are criminals, Alana, I'm not going to let you."

Alana activated her taser. "You won't have to." Since they were crawling, he just closed his eyes and lay down. She sat up and tased his friends from a distance. That was a gun she wasn't used to, but, if her calculations were right, they would wake up very soon. She feared leaving them unconscious in such a dangerous place, but a quick look told her that there was nobody around.

She took some distance and went to the other side of that place, so that she could descend on a hill where there were some bushes. Her aim was the bigger house. Perhaps Janet would be there. Before reaching the house, she looked at it from her higher position. There was always a way to enter. In this case, there was an energy generator on the roof. They would need a panel or a trapdoor to access it. Alana hid in the shadows, dashing in silence from point to point until she climbed to that roof and hid in the shadow of the generator. As much as there were guards all around the area, they seemed relaxed and not paying much attention. She doubted they'd spare a moment to look twice at shadows.

There was a panel leading below, but Alana didn't have her tools. She could perhaps snap it, but the sound could attract some attention. She decided to look for an alternate entry. There it was: on the second floor there was a window with outer bars, but open. Alana climbed the wall and peeked inside. It was an empty, dark room. The bars weren't wide enough to prevent Alana from coming through.

It looked like a regular bedroom, with a double bed and some other objects. Outside there was a hallway and stairs. Alana listened. People tended to be noisy. Either their breath, or their steps, or the shuffling of objects could tell where they were. They were all downstairs now. Perhaps Alana could search the rooms and see if she found the sphere. No, that would be stupid. First, she wasn't sure if Mara was even there, and second, the woman would probably keep the sphere close by. She walked towards the stairs and heard voices.

A man said, "There's no need to hurry this."

"But there's no need to wait!" A woman replied. Alana's hairs shivered before she even realized that the voice belonged to Mara. The woman continued, "I have complete control over the creatures, and I think we can get started soon."

Alana risked a peek. Mara talked to a man while clutching something on her right hand—the sphere!

There were also two security guards standing by the door. Alana had a taser, but it didn't work from such a large distance. If she descended the stairs, by the time she got down, one of the guards would have already shot her, and she doubted they had taser guns. Those were killing guns.

But the sphere was there. The sphere! With it, she would be able to do anything she wanted. The guards were near the door, though. They weren't expecting a threat to come from the inside. She needed to get closer to them but the stairs wouldn't do.

Alana went back to that bedroom, got out, and climbed down. She went around the building to the closest window to the room where she'd seen Mara and the man. The glass was down. Bad luck. Well, there was something she could do.

She tapped on the window twice, then lay down as close to the wall as she could. The men would need to open the window to see her. Indeed, that was exactly what they did, and Alana was fast; tased them both, tased the man coming in her direction, and was about to push up the window to climb in, when she saw Mara walking towards her.

Slightly out of range for the taser, but it would have to do. Alana activated it. Nope, it didn't do. While Mara knelt to pick up a gun, Alana entered the room, ran towards the woman, and activated the taser from up close.

Mara laughed. Alana felt her stomach drop but tried again. Nothing.

The woman continued laughing "I'm immune to those tricks, child!"

Alana took the opportunity to kick the gun out of Mara's hand, dash to the table, grab the golden sphere, and make for the door.

"Janet, help me save myself."

Janet replied in her ear. "I still can't obey you."

Alana didn't have time to protest or try to understand it, she ran towards a dragon pen. Mara was out of the door and screamed, "Alert!"

Right. She was going to be shot by the guards in the towers. To her surprise, nothing happened, though. Wow, those guards were even lazier than she'd suspected.

Someone walked towards them. Jasper! Perhaps he'd tased the guards on the towers.

He said, "Mother. Stop."

Mara still laughed. "I'm armed, and you aren't."

Two people came running from the house. Ugh, so there were more people inside.

"Hold him!" Mara said.

Jasper stood his ground, which was stupid, he could have run, and the two guards grabbed his arms.

Meanwhile, Alana ran towards Mara and grabbed the woman's weapon. It shot the air, then the woman grabbed it back and threw it far away.

"I don't need those trinkets."

Great, because on a one-to-one fight, Alana would have

the advantage since she was fast. That said, Jasper was looking, and she wondered whether she'd be able to hurt the woman in front of him.

While Alana hesitated, Mara stepped away from her, closed her eyes, spread her arms wide and yelled, "Kill her!"

There was a roar behind Alana. The closest dragon jumped his pen and ran towards her. Now, running to escape would be useless. Alana ran towards Mara. If the woman was really controlling the dragon—and that was what it looked like—she would make it stop once Alana was too close to her.

But Alana couldn't reach the woman, as if there were an electric field around her. Everything else happened in less than a second, but that was not how her mind registered it. Mara kept her eyes closed and hands raised. The dragon rushed towards Alana, stretching a claw. It would be a nicer death than if it spat his acid, so that was the thought in Alana's mind. She wanted one last look at Jasper, though.

Sweet Jasper, who'd helped her just because of his kindness. Yes, he was good looking and rich on top of that, but the warm feeling in Alana's chest had nothing to do with his looks or who he was. There was something wrong with him, though. The men still held his arms, but instead of struggling, like before, he had closed eyes and an expression very similar to his mother.

Alana crouched into a ball, hands over her head, but the dragon didn't touch her. Jasper let out a terrified scream, and she was sure this would be the moment of her death, but again nothing happened.

When Alana finally peeked, she saw Mara's body on the ground, her head ripped away. Dragons jumped away from their pens everywhere, and two of them held down the men who'd been holding Jasper. He knelt near his mother's body, weeping. Alana had no idea what to say. She wanted to run towards him and hug him, but at the same time, she feared he would be upset at her for causing his mother's death. Worse, from what she was gathering; she'd caused him to kill his own mother.

One of the men under a dragon's claw said, "Easy, easy. We just work here."

Jasper got up and ran to him, yelling at the top of his lungs, "You just work? You just work? People like you have these innocent creatures hurt because you can't think for yourselves."

"It's not that easy," the man said.

In his state of fury, the dragons were getting agitated. Soon Alana was underneath a claw.

Jasper stared in her direction and the dragon let her go. Alana whispered, hoping Janet would listen, "Any idea how I can make up for him?"

"It's not your job," Janet replied.

Even if it wasn't really an answer, Alana was glad to hear Janet's voice. Jasper sat on the ground and Alana decided to approach him. She knelt beside him and hugged him. "It was not your fault, it was an accident."

He shook his head. "It wasn't. I wanted to save you, even if..."

"You didn't do anything."

"Oh, yeah, I did. Don't take that away from me."

Alana just hugged him. Perhaps anything she said would only make matters worse. Jasper hugged her back, leaning his chin on her shoulder. Alana looked to the side, fearing guards or the men who'd been in the house. She wasn't sure how long she'd tased them for. There were also the two men. The dragons had released them, but they just looked in their direction as if thinking what to do.

"Jasper," Alana whispered. As much as she knew he needed time to grief, this was not the right moment.

He got up and spoke out loud, "I have two friends who are coming with the Alliance Police. Now, you may think you have a deal with the police, but you don't have a deal with me. I'm Jasper Forin and I succeed my mother in the Alliance. You were just working, that's fine. Help us. Give us information and we will free you. Either way, you don't want to hurt me or her, because my friends will know."

The guards threw their weapons down and raised their hands. Alana wasn't sure if it was because of his little speech or his momentary control of the dragons. Perhaps both?

Another man walked towards them, hands up. "I don't know what's happening here, but I got a request to bring my transporter to this place. I didn't even know there was a port here. They said you had livestock to transport."

Alana looked at Jasper. "You're going to take the dragons away?"

He shook his head. "The guards and everyone else who works here."

One of the guards protested, "Somebody needs to feed them, though."

Jasper shook his head. "They can hunt—once these towers preventing them from leaving are deactivated. But we can bring back essential personnel—once they've been interrogated."

———

ALANA SAT BACK on the ship. This time she was traveling to Ringon and didn't have to hide in a tiny box. Jasper was going to assume his seat in the Alliance, while Alana was going to use her remaining precious stones—which had been found among Mara's things—to start a new life. She had no idea what life, though. For so long she'd dreamed about leaving, and yet, she'd never stopped to think about what she would do after she left Samitri. Now there were too many painful thoughts in her mind for any decision.

Jasper had been quiet and somber, even a little distant. They'd successfully arrested and interrogated the people who'd been working at that strange dragon complex, but they didn't know anything. The man who'd been found with Mara had been the governor and was arrested as well.

Janet hadn't spoken since then. Perhaps Mara had done something weird with the sphere.

"I know why they were keeping the dragons." Jasper stared straight ahead.

"Why?"

"Customs inspection can find weapons. They wouldn't know how to distinguish between laskis and dragons."

"So she could attack any planet."

He nodded. Talking about his mother like that was odd, but all the evidence indicated that she'd been the mastermind of the operation. They still had no idea why she'd done it and if she'd been working within an organization.

At least the dragons had been freed, although still contained within the valley, and the area was going to receive more attention. Martel and Gala had been nominated interim governors, but the truth is that they longed to return to the Faris forests. Jasper was going to take his seat and then decide what to do with Samitri, since it had been in his mother's jurisdiction.

Alana wanted to ask him how he'd controlled the dragons, but she feared upsetting him. Perhaps he'd forget it and convince himself that he hadn't done anything. Alana couldn't forget his expression, though. She'd always thought this kind of power had been the stuff of legend. Well, she'd also always thought that handsome, kind, young men who were interested in poor damsels was the stuff of stories. Well, that said, nothing like matricide to put a damper on romance.

They went separate ways in Ringon. She also had her fake identity and credits back, so she made it to the heart of

Ringon City and found a hotel. As she sat on her bed, she heard Janet's voice.

"Alana?"

Finally. "Where have you been?"

"I only work when you are alone," Janet replied.

"I had my own room, though."

"You were still too close to Jasper."

"I see. So, are you still bound to Mara?"

"No, but that's only because she was killed. She used powerful words binding me to her until her death."

Alana took the sphere so that she could look at the small woman. "But she'd eventually run out of her three wishes, wouldn't she?"

Janet shook her head. "Her wishes were unlimited."

"Oh. Because of her words?"

"Because her first wish had been to have unlimited wishes."

Alana felt really stupid. How come she hadn't thought of that? And the whole reason she hadn't chosen to flee Samitri with her mother as her first wish was because she was rationing the wishes and believed a huge amount of money would allow her to get most of the things she wanted. How wrong she'd been.

"You said you needed help, that what she wanted to do was beyond the worst imaginable. Can you tell me what it was?"

"Not really, but it had to do with knowledge that shouldn't be accessible to humans."

Alien, ancient power. If legends were true, and now she

was pretty close to believing they were, Mara could have been unstoppable.

"I guess I'm glad you no longer work for her, then."

Janet exhaled, as if in relief. "So am I."

"Was it her natural power or you who allowed her to have such strong control over the dragons?"

"Both, maybe. I told her how to do it, but she had it in her."

"How could Jasper do it, then?"

"I don't know. He must have had that power and unlocked it at that moment."

What a horrible moment. She wasn't sure if Janet was someone who could give advice, but it was the only person Alana had. "Do you think he'll forgive me?"

"No."

She sounded certain. Alana understood it, but still, she'd hoped to hear something different, but then, what was the point in feeding false hopes?

Janet added, "He has nothing to forgive you for. It was his choice. It was his mother's choice to try to kill you in front of him. It was his mother's choice to allow children to be killed, to kill Leah and Mike in front of him. Perhaps it was the only way he could stop it. If you had died, he'd also feel responsible."

"But it wouldn't have been his fault."

"That's not how people think, though. Don't you think it's your fault your mother died?"

"In my case it was. I was so stupid."

Janet shook her head. "It wasn't your fault."

Alana then stared at the little woman. "Janet, do you have anyone, or any, uh, something you love?"

The small woman looked down.

"Are you lonely in this sphere?" Alana asked. "Have you been lonely for hundreds of years?"

Janet's voice was tight. "Time passes differently for us."

"What are you? Why are you in this sphere?"

"Why do you think?"

Alana had no idea. "I don't know."

"Imprisoned."

An enormous feeling of guilt took over Alana. "Really? You should have told me. I'd never used you. I mean—"

"It's fine. How could you have known? I was serving you."

"Can I set you free?"

"Don't you want your two remaining wishes?"

Alana thought about it. She had considered maybe asking for a way to get close to Jasper, but it would be so wrong. Plus, she couldn't risk having Janet in the wrong hands again. "I don't want the wishes. I want you free. How can I do it?"

The sphere shone, and a bright white light came from it. Janet grew to the size of a regular human, maybe a smaller than average human, like Alana, and said, "Thank you."

"All I had to do was ask how to free you?"

"No. You had to give up on having me helping you achieve your wishes. Your greatest wish had to be seeing me free."

Alana shrugged. "I'm glad I did it, then. You should have told me."

"I couldn't."

Alana felt a pang in her chest to lose her only remaining friend. "I'll miss you."

"I'll stop by."

"Aren't you going to the far galaxy where your people live?"

"We are not like you. We can be everywhere. I'll stop by. Now take it easy."

The little woman disappeared. Alana was completely alone. She lay on her bed, wondering if she should contact Jasper. Would he want to see her after all that happened? She wasn't sure. After a while, a light flickered on the panel beside the bed, and an automated voice said, "Message for the Black Mouse."

Her heart sped up. Should she refuse it, say she had no idea who that person was? She sighed. "Pass it through."

A written message came on the screen, saying:

For a long time, we watched you retrieve classified information in Samitri. Not all the work was done for us, but some of it was. We had you investigate Jasper's ship, but the culprit was his mother. We know what you did against Mara. If you are interested in fighting more battles like that, talk to our contact. Pay attention to a codename given to you by a friend. Somebody will contact you. We don't pay well, but it's for a higher cause.

Higher cause? That was all that she needed; a reason to keep going. Codename given by a friend? What could it be, though? Jack-in-the-box. So Flick, Angel, or both were also in this organization. Could she trust a piece of anonymous information? Well, she would need to see. That said, it was annoying that she didn't know when or where they would contact her. The message faded from the screen.

Alana found a small restaurant to eat, then came back to the hotel. In her room, a light flickered, and the artificial voice said, "Visitor for Alana. Let in, or meet downstairs?"

Her heart sped up. It was probably her contact. "Downstairs," she said. No way a stranger would be allowed in her room.

She rushed downstairs and saw Jasper. He had a shy smile. "I was in the area, then I saw you enter here. I was wondering if you'd like to go out for dinner."

It was more likely that he'd accessed some information and found where she was, but she let it slide. "Now?"

"Yeah, I—"

"Sure!" She'd just eaten, but she feared wasting that opportunity.

ALANA ATE CRUNCHY, green leaves like she'd never had before. She could eat this stuff twice, three times, forever.

Jasper looked at her. "Listen, I was thinking something."

She swallowed. "What?"

"The dragons. Samitri. We can't leave them."

"Aren't Martel and Gala there?"

"Not for long. I know you may have some trauma, some bad memories from that planet, but at the same time, you could help me make it a better place, not only for the dragons, but for the people—if you want to."

Alana wasn't sure what he was saying. Was he inviting her to go back to Samitri? She asked something else, "What about the seat in the Alliance?"

"We meet once a month. Most of them live in different planets. They all have their little secrets. I don't need to be here all the time."

Alana considered. "Well, if you want to do something good, and if you think I can help you... Sure, why not?"

"Can we leave next week?"

Alana was astonished. "Yes."

He smiled. She didn't want to ask him if he wasn't too traumatized to return there because she feared he could change his mind. In a way, that was an excellent opportunity to get close to him again, even if she wasn't sure what exactly he wanted her to do over there.

They walked slowly back to the hotel. Alana was still fascinated by all the different buildings, the suspended rails everywhere, and the bustle of such a huge city. But it had never been Ringon that she wanted, but freedom, hope. They stopped near the door.

She asked, "Why me, though?"

He stared at her. Alana could get lost in those kind blue eyes. He took her hand, pulled her closer, and kissed her. She had no idea how much she'd been longing for this, how strange it had been not to be kissing him, how good she felt when this close to him.

Beneath all his sadness there was so much love, longing, and more. Perhaps his hair didn't look like clouds now, but he could make her feel like she was on clouds. And that was what mattered; being with someone she loved.

———

JASPER WAS glad that his natural hair had grown back. He and Alana had a lot of work. He mostly cared for the Dragon Valley, trying to deactivate the unnecessary disruption towers and make sure the creatures were healing. He didn't get too close to them except when he had some equipment and calming gas. Whatever had happened that tragic night, it wasn't something he could replicate. He was glad he'd been able to save Alana despite the terrible price.

Alana was really good at negotiating with farm owners. She and Jasper couldn't try to do anything too sudden and couldn't cross the powerful people on the planet, but slowly they could change things there. Very soon tourism would pick up again, and Samitri would maybe become the prosperous planet it once had been.

They sometimes visited Ringon; he, for the Alliance meetings. He had to sit with greedy, evil people and pretend nothing was wrong. Alana for her part had her little tasks for the Rising Horizon, an organization that should be secret, especially from people in the Peace Alliance, but Alana didn't want to keep secrets from him. Maybe one day they'd get to know him better, and they could work together for a better Human Universe. They were starting with Samitri.

. . .

THE END

————

WANT to read more books in the same universe? *Star Fire* is set 12 years later, in a different planet in the neighbouring galaxy.

dayleitao.com/books/star-fire

A PLANET and its moon are in war with each other.

Saytera has been separated from the life she's always known. Her only strength is her mediocre knowledge of magic. It won't take her far in Academy 7.

On the moon, Dess has become the best pilot he could be, but it is not enough for him to be accepted to Command Training. He'll have to fly a new path—and risk his life on a regular basis by coming to the planet, in enemy territory.

A NOTE FROM DAY LEITAO

I hope you enjoyed Alana and Jasper's story. You can always email me and let me know what you think at day@sparkly-wave.com

I write fantasy, sci-fi, and often a mix of both. You can get updates and freebies by signing up to my mailing list at http://dayleitao.com

www.ingramcontent.com/pod-product-compliance
Lightning Source LLC
Chambersburg PA
CBHW021731190726
48288CB00009B/2999